ULTIMA THULE

Ultima Thule
The Life of an Island Daughter

RHONA RAUSZER

edited by Linda Williamson

First published in Great Britain in 2005 by
Polygon, an imprint of Birlinn Ltd
West Newington House
10 Newington Road
Edinburgh
EH9 1QS

www.birlinn.co.uk

ISBN 10: 1 904598 36 6
ISBN 13: 978 1 904598 36 7

The publishers acknowledge subsidy from the

Scottish
Arts Council

towards the publication of this volume.

British Library Cataloguing-in-Publication Data
A catalogue record for this book is available
on request from the British Library

Typeset by Hewer Text UK Ltd, Edinburgh
Printed and bound by Thomson Litho, East Kilbride

To my husband Kazik
non omnia moria bunter

Contents

Acknowledgements

With thanks to Linda, known to me as Minnehaha, for bearing with me; and to Christine for bringing peat to my fire.

Thanks also to Christine Martin for use of the following photographs – 'Rhona at home, 2004' and 'Portrait of Rhona by Frank T Copnall' – and to Bryan & Shear Ltd for 'Rhona and Kazik aboard *Pythagoras*'.

Editor's Note

Ultima Thule: The Life of an Island Daughter is Rhona Rauszer's autobiography, an oral narrative composed and recorded by herself over a period of twelve years between 1992 and 2004. The sound recordings, cassette tapes, were transcribed by friends on the Isle of Skye who assisted the author in her blindness.

Christened Mairianna Beathag, Rhona Rauszer is called after her mother and maternal grandmother (Rebecca) of the MacLeod and MacKinnon clans, south Skye. Although she was born in Liverpool and spent more than a third of her life away from the island, no place to the author's mind could be more of a home than Skye (see plate 22).

About her childhood in Cheshire, she has said: 'Hoylake is really a seaside resort, and, in those early days, it was very quiet and a very pleasant place to live in. I loved it almost as much as Skye, but that's an exaggeration, because who could love anything as much as one loves Skye.' Rhona's life story, *Ultima Thule*, is told here with a continuous reference to the imagination, that is, as fact based on fiction. And her second volume of short stories, *The Light Fantastic: Skye Folk and Fantasies*, published simultaneously with *Ultima Thule*, illustrates the inversion of this work – a life of fiction based on fact. Truth is a complementary picture of both.

By the time Mairianna MacLeod gives birth to Rhona in chapter two of the autobiography, a character is created, Sophia Maria, who reveals the author's more intimate feelings and experiences as a child. (The English equivalent of 'Beathag' in an old Gaelic dictionary was 'Sophia', which was adopted by Rhona as her by-name.) The technique of the frame (a story that contains another story) in literature is very old, a structural feature of earliest Sanskrit collections. Characters within the main story tell their own stories, become narrators; and the narrator herself becomes a character. Life is one with drama; events unfold and relate to the whole like branches to the trunk of a tree. Rhona's original narration, the frame of *Ultima Thule*, was composed with directives to insert her previously written short stories at key points. The prose is thereby enlightened with imaginary tales, poetry and diary extracts, written before the onset of Rhona's blindness in the 1980s.

Ultima Thule has had a special meaning for Rhona since the end of her married life in Richmond with Kazik, inventor and World War II veteran. Throughout her professional life, as a child of the Isle of Skye and direct descendant of Gaelic forbears, Rhona would feel a certain emptiness – an edge of impossibility – when she was living apart from the island:

> One thing about being alone in London, I always knew that I could drop everything and go to Euston Station and get the train back home to Skye. I always knew I had Skye behind me, and the life there was such a contrast; and it was so refreshing to smell the peat once more and the bog myrtle in the hills and hear the sheep bleating. And not only the sheep bleating, but the people, their voices and the Gaelic language. I had inherited a great love for this way of life. And our family in Broadford were very happy . . .

'The North' became an anchor in a far-flung life of courage and adventure; 'amazing endurance' was A P Herbert's commendation for her naval service in the war.

Granted the opportunity to work with Rhona as her editor

has been nothing short of an honour. The help of Neil MacGregor and Richard Blose in the preparation of the typescript is gratefully acknowledged. And to David Campbell, true friends are like gold.

Linda Williamson
Edinburgh, 2005

Tangle and Weed

The harvest was being brought in late that year, the weather having been atrocious. All the villagers had come together to help each other get the sodden stuff in. It must have been very hard on them, as you felt you had to lend a hand whether you were well or ill, and Rebecca MacLeod was far from well. In fact, she was about to deliver her baby and should have stayed at home – but it made her feel guilty and she thought she had time to come and give a hand. So that's how my mother Mairianna NicLeoid was born in the field; the women circled round about Rebecca using their skirts and aprons to shield the delivery of this tiny little child.

Mairianna was born in 1884 the daughter of Angus and Rebecca MacLeod, née MacKinnon. She lived with her nine brothers and sisters in a tiny cottage in Breakish, the Isle of Skye and walked daily three miles to Broadford to school. She walked at the side of the road because that was softer on her bare feet. Her shoes were slung over her shoulders; they were for some very special occasion that might turn up in the future, far too good to be worn!

Rebecca MacLeod had a hard job accommodating all ten of her children – she was like the old woman who lives in a shoe and didn't know what to do. However, she did know what to do and she farmed her children out for sleeping at night, some of them that is. And that is how Mairianna and her younger brother Neil came to go and stay at night with their mother's brother, Uncle Donald, who lived in an enchanting thatched cottage, full of smoke and atmosphere. Donald MacKinnon was quite a character, had a little beard and spoke no English, or very little; he hated the language and didn't make any attempt to use it. He didn't make any attempt to do any work either! He just sat in his little cottage and was perfectly content. There was a little river at the side of the house and some huge, ancient trees, which unfortunately in later years were sawn down.

Donald may have used some of the wood of his trees to make his own furniture, because everything was hand-made: little stools and chairs, quaint and lop-sided, the big, long trust and little tables and chests. The fire was more or less in the middle of the room with great stones all around it, and a cauldron with soup, and the smoke was all drawn up through a canopy into the ceiling – a big, hand-stitched leather canopy – and there was a loft alongside that, before you got as far as the chimney. He used to pretend that it was full of children, lost boys, so to speak, rather like J M Barrie's. He told extraordinary stories and used to entertain about twenty people of an evening just with his tales.

One of them was about the doctor coming to see him and he had pleurisy or something in his chest: and the doctor said he would have to have a poultice on his chest, 'Now will you do that, Donald?'

And Donald said, 'Yes,' he would do that, he would put a poultice on his chest, but he didn't see what on earth good that would do.

So about a week later the doctor came to see him again and said, 'Well, Donald, are you feeling any better? Did you put the poultice on your chest?'

'Yes, there it is, you can see it for yourself, and damn all good it did me!' he said; because he had mixed a poultice and put it on the wooden blanket chest that he had made himself – thought that was what the doctor had meant.

Storytelling seemed to run in the MacKinnon family, and the women were as well known as the men for their works of imagination. Rebecca gave this one based on an old Gaelic air to the song collector Mrs Kennedy Fraser:

> Tangle and weed I weave thee
> Close to the rocks I cleave thee

Màiri hummed the mournful tune to herself. Sadly, she raised herself from the edge of the tide where she'd been gathering whelks and decided to stop. She would shout to her sister Kirsty who was away out on the far stretch of sandy shore. When people worked in those days in the fields and on the shore they didn't talk to each other, they shouted. In fact, some of the men joked about it, 'If you wanted to shout to somebody from Plockton, they could hear you in Strathcarron!' But of course I don't think that would be possible.

So, Màiri gathered up her belongings and started to walk and walk and walk. She decided to plough her way up Sìthshader hill till she would reach the edge of the forest. Continuing along the steep waggly path that the sheep had made, exhausted and tired and oh so miserable, she leaned her back against a silver birch and listened to the birds in the thick of the forest. She thought she heard a cuckoo – that was like her – cuckoos stole other people's nests and settled in them. Is this not what she had done? The tears flowed from her eyes as she thought about it, and trickled down the side of her nose till they reached the edge of her lips. She could taste them. They were salty of course, like a salt herring.

Although it was yet quite early, clouds were forming, a distant clap of thunder jerked her into activity. She would go down the hill again and join the others. She could see in the distance that Tormod . . . Oh God, that name, that man! Had her grandmother not warned her, 'No matter how handsome a man is,' she had said, 'take a look at his neck. If he has a thick neck, have nothing to do with him!'

Well, she never wanted to have anything to do with him; he was her sister's man, they were betrothed and they loved each other. What could she do, what could she say? She would have to go away, she would have to run away somewhere. But where to go, she's never been more than twelve miles away from home in her life!

When she reached the shore again she could see this beautiful panoramic view, three dimensional; in the foreground rugged outcrops of rock, and in the centre ground Tormod filling his cart with seaweed, children cluttering round crying for a ride. They would only get their bottoms wet climbing onto the cart and sitting on the seaweed, but he was moving off now. The children would go to their own homes, and no doubt stand in front of a peat fire and get their torrnaigs warmed and their trousers dried before their mothers would come in from the milking. In the far distance there was her sister Kirsty silhouetted against the darkening sky, she looked almost like Bride. Màiri, tall and dark, was totally different in appearance: Kirsty was short and fair with long golden hair. Kirsty did not seem to be alone. There was a cailleach with her, well known, a bit scatty, her name was Cartogena. She called herself a poetess and wrote some quite amusing poems. She could also tell

4

fortunes, what you call a speywife. Màiri walked out to join them in the whelks, but, as she did so Kirsty moved further along the shore.

The old woman and Màiri worked away, gathering whelks off the big leaves like umbrellas that grew out of the sand, tall and unattainable except on a very low tide, like rhubarb leaves, and enormous whelks were found there. The cailleach was beginning to get annoyed with Màiri – being young and energetic she was able to gather far more whelks into her sack than Cartogena – so she started to be a wee bit nasty and said, 'Oh well, you'd better stop now, because you've got a lot of worry ahead of you. This very night there will be a change in your life. And you will be going far away soon, far, far away, to another country. You'll not be alone, but you'll be hanging your head in shame and your heart will be heavy. Mark my words!'

Màiri said, 'Oh, duin do bheul' in Gaelic (which means, shut your gob, don't talk nonsense). But the cailleach said, 'What I say is true: before the nettles wither in the field you'll be in a far distant place. Mark my words!'

So Màiri lifted her sack and started to come back towards the machair, the shore and her sister. Little did Kirsty know what Màiri was going to tell her. The sun was going down and thundery clouds were forming. Màiri was now exhausted with fear and anxiety, and in such a state she didn't know what on earth she could do, when Kirsty approached her. She was not knowing how she could tell her but tell her she must, because through time Kirsty would know. She was in an impossible predicament and a very bad temper, having quarrelled with Cartogena, not believing a word the old fool had said.

Màiri was trying to be civilised and started telling as best she could, and as gently what had happened: it was hard to confess to being pregnant, how Tormod had abused her – and cheated on them both. Kirsty's attitude when she was told was most peculiar. She never said a single word. She was as though she had been struck dumb. In fact, she looked odd. Her eyes seemed to have gone back in her head and were showing the whites. Màiri thought she was going to have a fit, but instead of that Kirsty collapsed, in a dead faint. Màiri sat beside her and tried to revive her. But there was nothing happening, and she thought Kirsty was dead. She felt terrible – what had she done, had she killed her sister? She panicked and shook Kirsty with all her might, and shouted at her, 'For God's sake, get better, don't die on me!' Fundamentally she loved her sister, it was a sort of love-hate relationship. But Màiri had to do something, she couldn't let Kirsty go home . . . well, how could she go home if she was dead?

So, all she could think of was making her fast to the machair reeds that grew profoundly all around her head. She took hold of Kirsty's golden hair and tied it to the seaweed and the reeds. She didn't know why she was doing this, she hadn't a clue. Perhaps because part of the time she was hating her and wanting her never ever to come back home again. And in this way, if she secured her, the tides which were coming in now would sweep her out to sea or at least drown her and Màiri's guilt would be covered. Now what should she do herself? She couldn't go home either. So she ran after Tormod, but he'd already gone.

He had taken the seaweed up to Màiri's croft and returned their father's cart and horse. He hadn't time to spread the seaweed: he too felt a terrible guilt in his heart because of what he had done to the two sisters. So he made his way home, to his croft; it had been left to him by an uncle. His parents were dead, and he had quite a bit of money. He also had of all things a whisky still hidden away at the old fank across the river. He decided to go up there, collect some of his whisky samples, run off the following day to Gourock or Greenock and negotiate the sale of his whisky.

So, kicking off his wellington boots, he made to cross the river. He loved to feel the river, especially when it was in spate, running between his toes as he stepped like a child from one to the other of the huge granite stones that reached across, then made his way to the fank. It was an exciting place, an ancient fank never used now, overgrown with hazel bushes, hidden by them, an ideal place for his whisky stores. Some of the bottles were in barrels, hidden in by meal and cow food and all sorts of things. He would give a whistle to his cousin in the next croft and tell him to look after things while he was away. And then he will see if he could find Màiri, try to find out whether Kirsty knew or not of his deception.

Màiri meanwhile, completely demented, paced backwards and forwards wringing her hands. She didn't know what on earth she could do. She would have to get away. And then, she conceived the idea that if Tormod didn't know what she had done, she need never tell him. It was fair enough; she would have to live with the guilt of her crime for the rest of her mortal days, since he had deceived them both. She would go to him and suggest that they very quickly elope. It was not unusual in those days – it was much cheaper, save killing off about twelve or fifteen hens, and perhaps a bullock for the wedding. Usually the parents were extremely glad when their daughters decided to run away, especially with an eligible young man such as Tormod.

So looking up the hill she thought she saw a fire blazing on top of the hillock. But it wasn't a fire, it was a huge bush of gorgeous yellow gorse. And it came into her mind that Moses might well have mistaken what he supposed was a fire for this brilliant, blazing crop of gorse, if gorse grew on Mount Sinai – of this she had no knowledge. But she did know that he had brought down the Commandments. When she thought about the Commandments and thought about what she'd done, she screamed aloud in an agony of remorse and then began to run to her house. Her mother would still be at the milking. She would leave a note for her to say she and Tormod were leaving together that very same night. She would gather her few belongings and race up to Tormod, tell him nothing and the pair of them would elope.

Tormod was mightily relieved to see her, because he now realised how much he loved her. They busied themselves harnessing up his horse and fixing his gig, filling it with provisions and their belongings. And off they went on their long journey to Gourock where they hoped they could sell the horse and the gig. He had, as I said, some money put aside and they would set sail on one of the ships for Canada. He didn't know where the ship they would choose would land, and they didn't care, so long as they got away. As Cartogena had foretold, they would hang their heads in shame and try to live with the ghastly deeds they had performed for the rest of their mortal days.

As they rode along they frequently looked back across the shimmering sea, the sun making a Jacob's ladder shine in a straight line towards them. The surface of the water was glistening, putting in mind an enormous sea trout, its scales all shimmering and dancing in the evening light. They would never be able to return.

Tangle and weed I weave thee
Close to the rocks I cleave thee

so ran the old song, and that is also the end of my story

By 1895 Mairianna MacLeod was growing up fast, becoming a tall, slim, skinny girl with long, dead straight, pitch black hair, and her eyes were a light blue, forget-me-not blue – very strange really, and she had a very pale skin (see plate 2). And although she wasn't delicate, she looked delicate. In Broadford School the pupils had to carry with them a peat for the fire, plus a tiny little, oval-shaped Coleman's mustard tin containing some sugar. Mairianna and her brothers were all quite clever, one brother in particular – Duncan. Mairianna herself was good at maths and also good at any artistic efforts she would make; she used to paint on wooden boxes.

There used to be a visiting schoolmaster who taught them and he came over from Ireland, his name was Mr Shevass, and I think he became quite famous later on in life. He was a Sinn Feiner, of course, and stayed quite a lot of his life in the summer in Skye, and taught the children sometimes in an empty shed with straw on the floor. They would all sit cross-legged and he would teach them how to paint and draw, and a lot of extra subjects that they didn't get in school.

Before going on to Broadford School many children started their education in Breakish School. It was an interesting place with outside lavatories: a row of about six little huts, lined up above a small river. It was fascinating to sit on a little wooden seat, and through the hole see the water gushing past – the river took everything nasty and smelly away – and of course kept these little lavatories very clean. You could drop little bits of paper, little ships down inside this round hole and watch them being washed away as though they were going to sea.

The headmaster they had in the 1890s, in Mairianna's days, was very strict indeed, and used to punish the young boys a lot if they came late. He had a tawse hanging on the wall, but had the vicious habit of making the boys take their trousers down, laying the boys across a desk and thrashing them with the tawse – after he had warmed it up in a pot of burgundy which he afterwards drank himself – or perhaps he drank it before he strapped the boys, in order to give his arms sufficient strength! I think it must have been a dreadful experience and probably affected them for the rest of their lives.

Across the road from the school in Breakish was a tiny, thatched cottage with a low chimney full of smoke and very, very dark inside; an old woman called Anna Cameron and her brother lived there. It was low enough for the children to clamber up, grabbing a hold of the stones and ropes that held the thatch together on the roof. They would shout, shove cabbages down the chimney and cause an awful smoke inside. Poor old Anna would come rushing out, choking, and she was known for always complaining of indigestion, 'Oh mar a tha mise leis a'ghaoith', she would say (oh, how I am with the wind). With her stick she would shout at the children and chase them for all she was worth.

It was not all that long before Mairianna's brothers grew old and strong enough to start building a new house on the croft for their mother. They started from the foundation – quite a large house – four of them at it diligently, John, Neil, Dan and Jimmy. All worked hard until they completed it. The new house, although large and roomy, had no proper sanitation. There was a wooden shed at the side attached to the gable end. It consisted of a little round wooden seat with a pail inside. I'm not very sure who was detailed off to empty that pail, but it was taken down the croft and buried inside an old ruined house or barn; one knew this is where the family slop pails were emptied because the nettles grew in abundance, and this is a very good sign. It was rather like a graveyard, a bit sinister. Inside the house, of course, under every bed there would be a beautifully designed chamber pot, porcelain at that. These were collected every day into the slop pails and it would be the job of the little maid, whoever she might be, to carry these downstairs. Afterwards the men would dispose of them in the aforesaid graveyard.

Mairianna was about sixteen at this time and grand old Uncle Donald had gone to work on the new railway line from Strome Ferry; he was in on the building of that and eventually they put trains on it. There was a great gala, a lot of the people from Skye, including Rebecca MacLeod, went to have the first ride in the first train from Strome Ferry to Kyle of Lochalsh. They were just wooden seats in open carriages and great smoke coming out of the engine; of course all the ladies were in their very best gear. Rebecca had a silk shawl on and a lovely bonnet, which her husband had bought on one of his sea trips to Salonica in Greece. It was a beautiful shawl and bonnet and she got it pretty well ruined with the smoke coming out of the coal-fired locomotive of the Highland Railway, as it was in those days. But she was very proud to have taken part in the first railroad into Kyle of Lochalsh.

Her husband Angus MacLeod was a quick-tempered, strict man but capable of being kindness itself if he chose. He was very strict with the children: in fact, if they were playing outside for too long or doing something that they perhaps shouldn't do, they used to go and get an old bodach whom they called the Toffee King. He used to give them toffees, and his name was MacKintosh; he would accompany them home so that their father wouldn't be too hard on them – stop Angus from taking the tawse down from the wall. It was a leather strap about a foot and a half long, sometimes longer, with four or five thongs on it. Angus would think nothing of thrashing the boys with this horrible leather strap, they were all very much afraid of it, and him, if he was in a bad temper.

But they didn't see all that much of him because he was nearly always at sea, sailing all over the world to America and Spain, and going round the Horn – he only came home really for very short spells in order to increase the size of his family. He had little to do with the upbringing of his large family. So poor old Rebecca had to make a living somehow, and the new house had an annexe built onto it she made into a shop. And, believe it or not, in the attic of this annexe she had a whisky still. She dealt in oatmeal and sugar, had sacks of this and that, and used to trade with the ships that came into the Broadford Pier; was known to walk all the way to Perth to transact her business.

Round about this time Angus MacLeod received a letter from solicitors in America; he was entitled to a large fortune, left to him by a relative, but he would have to go out to claim it himself. So of course this was tremendously exciting, because the family was very poor and it would be wonderful to get this money.

Angus persuaded a pal of his to go with him, and they embarked on a ship and off they sailed to America once more; but before they left the country Angus had been showing the letter around, and had shown it to a cousin on the mainland, a MacRae. This cousin did a very dirty trick, and Rebecca was never able to acknowledge any of the MacRae relations for the rest of her life she was so angry! Because this fellow MacRae beat Angus to it, and got to America first, pretended that he was Angus MacLeod and managed to get the inheritance! So when Angus arrived, there was a gang of men waiting for him, and making an attempt to kill him

He and his pal went to the hotel and they were having their first drink, when very wisely Angus thought there was something funny-looking about this whisky, 'I don't like the look of it at all.'

He is supposed to have thrown it into the fire, and it went up in multi-coloured flames. Angus was right in his suspicions, the drink was poisoned. So he and his pal decided to go somewhere else to eat and drink, and this they did. There was a gang of about twenty men waiting for him, they accosted Angus and his pal, cut his gallaces (or braces) and started fighting. But Angus and his pal were very strong, healthy men and they managed to escape. But they were very frightened indeed, they knew they would be killed and tried to make for their ship, got down to the quayside, and into the boat that had brought them over from the big ship. They started rowing back, but this gang of fellows got another boat and pursued them, capsizing them! So, the last bit of the adventure: Angus and his pal had to swim for the ship, and of course were safe enough when they got on board.

They didn't go ashore again in Savannah, and they got back to Britain, took the case up with British solicitors, but they never got anywhere with the case. And Angus never got any of the money. But from that day onwards there was no love lost between the MacRaes of Dornie and the MacLeods of Breakish.

Meanwhile, the MacLeods in Breakish were becoming a well-respected family (see plate 4). The oldest boy, Mairianna's brother Jimmy, was grown up and had decided he wanted to go in for the tailoring. He thought there would be quite a demand for clothes to be made round about Breakish and Broadford, so he contacted a friend of his in Liverpool, a Mr MacLean who was in the tailoring business. And off Jimmy went to Liverpool. He was there for quite some time, became a very expert tailor and thenceforth would be known as 'Seumas an Taillear'. He came back to Skye and transformed his mother's little shop into a tailoring establishment with a big, wide table on which he cut out trouser legs, jackets and sleeves for the local people. At first he was enthusiastic and made a very good job of a lot of the clothes, but gradually he got bored with the whole thing, got slower and slower. Eventually his clients would come in, have one leg of the trousers of the suit made, or a part of a waistcoat and say, 'Oh here now, I want that suit by tomorrow, I've got a funeral to go to and I've nothing to wear – for God's sake man, get that suit finished for me!'

Poor Jimmy hated being pressurised in that way, so he would stare at the one leg and wonder how he would get the energy to make the other. Eventually he got fed up and decided to convert the tailoring shop into a post office sorting office. When he wasn't out in his little shop cutting up his black twist tobacco with a huge penknife on the palm of his hand, he'd be indoors, in the kitchen in fact, where he had a beautiful roll-top desk, his pride and joy. There he would be acting as postmaster general, paying out postal orders and selling stamps, doing all the postal work for everyone round about. The biggest room in the house became the post office. They would come up from Lower Breakish, Upper Breakish and all around with their parcels, all kinds of goods and boxes of eggs. They were always sending away boxes of eggs and usually got them returned from relatives in Glasgow or Edinburgh filled with tomatoes – a great rarity, a tomato was just something very special in those days. And whoever had heard of an orange!

One of Jimmy's brothers, the much-loved John, was the exciseman in Broadford for a time in the old hall down by the limekiln (see plate 19). Another one, Neil, went to sea. Jimmy's older brother Malcolm was killed in the South African War of 1898–1902. The one who made the greatest name for himself was Duncan.

He really excelled himself, was quite a financial genius. He went to Glasgow at an early age, continued his studies at evening classes and went to many talks on various subjects, even spiritualism. At one of these talks he met a beautiful young lady from Arran, Isabelle MacNeil, who was deep into the suffragette movement. They courted each other while he was doing a job with a paraffin firm, but he took ill and in fact was sent home for a whole year. But he did not waste his time. He went back to the Broadford School, took extra lessons and furthered his education, preparing himself no doubt to go back to town and achieve his ambitions. After a spell in a bottling firm in Sheffield with a relation of his own, Duncan proceeded to go to Liverpool. He was already a businessman, involved in glass bottling, and had now connected himself with an Irish firm and a firm in Liverpool; started to make non-alcoholic drinks, realised there was a huge market for this in America. A railway engineer in Liverpool, Christopher Sykes, helped him immensely by introducing him to all the shipping companies in that city, and to contacts with road and rail transport. Christopher found digs for Duncan, helped him with his clothes, what to wear, introduced him to opera, took him around to concerts and introduced him to celebrities such as Dame Clara Butt.

Prohibition had now started in America and so Duncan MacLeod set sail for that country and did enormously well, starting off with the non-alcoholic drinks; and then coming back to this country, got introductions to the whisky brokers in Glasgow and elsewhere. He met up again with the pretty Isabelle from Arran and decided that he wanted to marry her. So he wrote home to Skye and invited his brother Jimmy and sister Mairianna to his wedding in Arran. And that's how Mairianna ventured forth from the Isle of Skye for the first time, wearing her good boots no doubt!

The wedding of Duncan MacLeod to Isabelle MacNeil from Arran was well remembered by those who attended. Mairianna and her brother Jimmy, Seumas an Taillear, travelled first to Glasgow and then south along the Clyde to get on board the ship for Arran. The ship was very full and it was rather a rough day. Mairianna decided to stay up on deck, when suddenly she was approached by a tall man in a frock coat and a top hat. Now Marianna had never seen anyone dressed like this before except the minister at home and sometimes the doctor; she had been told she must curtsey to them, be very polite.

So when this man came up to Mairianna and said, 'Hello, are you Duncan MacLeod's little sister?' she did a deep curtsey.

And Mairianna said, 'Yes, sir!' (Christopher Sykes used to laugh about that and say it was the only polite thing Mairianna ever said to him in his life thereafter.)

The wedding in Arran must have been a dreamlike affair, when you look at the photographs. They walked all the way from the house to the church in those days and had pipers preceding them. Belle MacNeil had many bridesmaids – sisters and cousins – all in beautiful flimsy dresses, and it was a hot, wonderful summer's day. Many photographs were taken and people talked about it in great detail.

After the wedding in Arran and the honeymoon was over, Uncle Duncan went back to Liverpool and bought a house in Highton, near a golf course. Christopher Sykes introduced him to the course where he made useful acquaintances. Soon there was a family on the way. Auntie Belle's first child was Ruby, and then there was Màiri and Angus. Belle was very much involved in pursuing the cause of the suffragette women, going to meetings and rallies; she didn't go as far as tying herself up in chains to the railings of the House of Commons, but she was a very active member of the Pankhurst suffragette set, was out a lot of the time, or had to be. So, Duncan got a bit worried and thought the ideal thing would be to get his sister Mairianna through from Glasgow to help his wife Belle.

After the wedding, Mairianna and Jimmy had stayed in Glasgow with very good friends from Skye, the Robertson family; Angus and his wife Rachel were most hospitable and didn't mind how long any Highlander stayed under their roof. They were kindness itself. They even wanted to teach Mairianna how to play the piano, as they were a very musical family, and taught her little things, like how to get onto a tramcar without breaking her neck. Mairianna was a very independent young woman and decided it wasn't really fair to stay on in Glasgow without contributing something to the household. Jimmy was going back to Skye and she flatly refused to go. She would take a job, any job. So she answered an advertisement for a housemaid in a big mansion. This job helped her to learn much that would come in very useful in later life: how to arrange flowers on a dining table, silver service, crystal and wines, working in the pantry under the butler's eye and a great many things in that household.

But it was extremely hard work! They worked from crack of dawn until after dinner at night, and well after midnight sometimes. She got exhausted and decided she would look for something easier, managed to get another job with Miss Raeburn, the famous artist's sister. She became a maid and liked it, found the paintings this lady had done and the artistic atmosphere very interesting. She began to learn quite a bit, then did a good deal of painting herself. She also learned how to crochet, do Italian quilt work; but eventually she got bored. One day walking along in the middle of Glasgow looking into the shop windows she came upon one called Ogg Brothers (later known as Coplands).

She pressed her nose to the window, was fascinated by the little wooden boxes flung across the ceiling in the shop on wires, scuttling here, there and everywhere and dropping down to a girl who would open out the little box, and take out change and money. This is where she wanted to work, so she opened the door and walked in, 'Please can I have a job here? I would love throwing these things across the ceiling.'

The lady laughed, 'Oh dear me, I don't know that you would get a job here – I mean, it's not very easy – you would have to see the manager up in the office.' This lady then asked, 'Where do you come from?'

And Mairianna said, 'I come from the Isle of Skye.'

The lady then said, 'Oh dear me, we'll have to do something about you,' and sent her up to the office. One of the Ogg brothers was there, he asked her about her background, where she came from and if she was good at arithmetic. It so happened that Mairianna was exceptionally good at arithmetic, so the Ogg brother gave her a list of figures to see how quickly she could add, which she did in no time at all. 'Well, you're on – start tomorrow morning!'

After a few weeks in the job brother Duncan in Liverpool got in touch with her, told her to come immediately, as his wife was having a very difficult time and they needed some help. Well, Mairianna protested naturally, as she was getting on very well in Ogg Brothers, getting early promotion and enjoying herself, had made many friends in Glasgow and didn't want at all to go down to Liverpool. Then she thought about Christopher Sykes, whom she really had admired and taken a bit of a fancy to, and thought perhaps she should go after all. She packed her wee tin trunk, travelled down and was met at the station by Duncan.

She looked charming and attractive, she always dressed well with a flair for colour and clothes. But when Duncan saw her tin trunk, all rusty at the edges, a horrible squashed trunk that had travelled with her all the way from Skye, he wouldn't allow it to be put in the taxi; but made arrangements for it to be delivered to his house by someone else. Mairianna felt very hurt about this; she had always found this little trunk very useful to sit on, especially in those days when she sailed from Armadale to Mallaig and rejoined a steamer that took her all the way steerage to Glasgow. In those days a lot of the people from Skye travelled by ship and the women used to huddle together in the steerage part of the boat. In order not to be accosted by amorous young men, they always had long hatpins with either a jewel or a lump of jet or a pearl on the end; this they didn't hesitate to use if any of the young men on board got too fresh with them.

However, her stay in Liverpool had its compensations as she had acquired two boyfriends – Christopher Sykes and a fellow called Willie Hay – rivals in seeking her hand in marriage. She used to string them along, have great fun in going out to skating rinks, concerts and the like. In the end, she got engaged to Christopher Sykes.

Meanwhile back in Skye, Angus MacLeod, her father, had died. And so Mairianna of course packed up the old tin trunk and travelled back home to comfort her mother, who was exceedingly distressed. This meant parting with Christopher Sykes, her fiancé for some three years. And then Christopher travelled up to Skye to claim his bride, there was a lovely wedding!

People, neighbours and friends, brought hens, marags (black and white puddings), lobsters, herring and everything you could imagine to the old Taigh Beathag (Rebecca's house) in Breakish. And there were dances in the hall in Broadford. When it came to the day of the wedding Mairianna must have looked exquisite in a beautiful, silk dress with inserts of big lovers' knots in lace embroidered all round the hem, and introducing here and there little bits of blue. She had several bridesmaids. I am told there were lanterns in all the trees, all the way between Breakish and Broadford Church, where she was to be married. And some of Christopher's friends came all the way from Liverpool to the Isle of Skye to attend the wedding. One particular fellow was called Bluffy Perch, quite a character, and they had enormous fun with him – he thought he was in no man's land – couldn't make out the way of life in Skye at all, it was such a novelty. However, they had pipers playing, walking ahead of the bride all the way to Broadford, and the service took place in the Church of Scotland.

Mairianna returned to Liverpool with her husband, Christopher, who had already prepared a house for her with quite a large garden full of apple trees which he tended regularly, putting lime on and hammering in a nail. I don't know the purpose of the latter, but I think it had something to do with rust helping the growth of the trees. And there was a greenhouse. Christopher had furnished the house mostly in the art nouveau style, although some precious antiques were given to him by his mother, one being a spinet piano brought all the way from Ireland. He also had some of the furniture specially made by a ship's carpenter for the house: there were two big armchairs with leather seats, fringes and brass studs holding that together, a beautiful Welsh dresser and a big dining table.

Oatcakes

Mairianna was soon pregnant but lost the first child; and then made herself quite ill by crawling out of bed and going to the window, on a bitterly frosty morning, to watch the tiny coffin being taken along the path to the gate and on to the hearse. Then I came along.

I am really the oldest of Mairianna's family, and so they were quite pleased to know that I was almost due. But mother, so thrilled and feeling so sure that she was nearly about to drop me, decided to get on the dining room table and do a wee Schottische, a Highland dance. Round and round she went – did she think this would bring on the baby a little quicker? But evidently they had been having supper with oysters, brown bread and butter and Guinness – would you believe it, Black Stout!

And there my mother was about to have me, when father raced off to get a midwife and found one called Mrs Tinkler, who came immediately. They weren't prepared with every-thing for me; they didn't have a cradle for instance, so father had a duet piano stool in oak, took the padded lid off and stuffed it with the necessary bedding for a new-born baby. That was my first cradle. Whether they thought this would make me inclined towards being a musical genius or not I don't know! (See plate 3.)

There were four other children added to Mairianna's family, two boys and two girls. Mairianna visited her Irish mother-in-law in Liverpool frequently and learned from her all the graces; the old girl was very strait-laced – in fact she was never known to lean forwards or backwards on a chair but always sat stark upright. She had a row of little white curls across her forehead and wore a linen cap. She always saw to it that Christopher, my father, practised his music diligently; so she got him up at five o'clock in the mornings to have half an hour's practice. Then he was allowed to go to Septon Park to skate on the ice, if there was any, and all this before going to work (see plate 20). And in the evenings, choir practice. That then is how my father became a very good singer and was a chorister in Liverpool Cathedral, the new one not yet fully built. Indeed, my mother would be often peeved when left alone in the evenings with her little babies whilst father went off 'swanning it', as she said, to the Philharmonic or a theatre where *The Gondoliers*, or some such performance was taking place. His deep bass voice was very useful, and it was during the times when Madame Patti and Dame Clara Butt were performing there.

Every year the whole family would board the train at Liverpool Lime Street, changing at Crewe, changing again at Perth, where we stayed the night with a very good friend of my mother's in the North British Hotel. And then on again the next day to Inverness and Kyle of Lochalsh and Skye. On one of these journeys I took very ill with whooping-cough, and as Duncan MacLeod had now moved back to Glasgow and had an enormous house, we all went there. Doctors were summoned, the best specialist in Glasgow and a night nurse and a day nurse.

This little girl called Sophia Maria was only three years old when War broke out in 1914. Her father had been left behind in the place called Cranford, now called Knutsford, because he was in charge of ammunition.

He worked for British Railways, and his job was to see to the transport of equipment for the War.

So, her mother decided the best thing to do was for them lock, stock and barrel to leave their father behind and travel up north to the Isle of Skye, where she was a native. But the unfortunate thing was that little Sophia Maria got ill before they reached Crewe, where they had to change for the North train. She had been holding her brother's hand, her little brother aged two: she held one hand and her mother held the other and they were rushing and so excited and so keen to get seats in the train – they ran either side of a lamp post and the poor little nipper got a horrible scar on his head. But the station master, a kindly man, managed to contact a doctor: the train was held up for at least ten minutes. The doctor okayed the child, put a dressing on him and they proceeded on their northward journey.

Then, catastrophe number two started: Sophia Maria started coughing and coughing and coughing; and it became obvious to her mother that she'd developed whooping cough, which was on the go at the time. So they decided to disembark from the train in Glasgow, because her mother had a brother who lived there. He had a very large mansion, was a very wealthy man, and she knew that he would be pleased to see them, would help with the child who was now coughing her guts out.

And poor little Sophia Maria got worse and worse, but she was very well attended, because she'd got a scar on her lung and had a heart condition as well. She needed very careful nursing. However, little by little she recovered and they were able to proceed to the Isle of Skye. Before leaving Glasgow I should describe the atmosphere there, at the beginning of World War I.

Troops were everywhere. And moving a lot in the middle of the night. So, little Sophia's nursery bedroom was prohibited to the rest of the family in case her little cousins, the twins, would also be infected by the whooping-cough. Poor little Sophia would lie there mostly alone, and she began to be very frightened, frightened of the dark, and she would get very panicky when she heard the soldiers in their big tackety boots marching along the main road en route for France or God knows where, singing their hearts out. All kinds of early wartime songs.

The night nurse would sing one, 'Land of hope and glory, mother wash me clean.' And the day nurse would sing half in English and half in Gaelic, because she came from Lewis in the Outer Isles:

> Around the corner behind the tree
> The sergeant major made love to me;
> Chaidh ticki tacki leis an oifisear
> Às an ar-til-ler-y.*

She was very religious, too, and used to help the cook; Sophia's uncle and aunt wondered why the twins, who were very young, just babies, always started to yell and cry and cry all weekend. Till at long last they discovered that the holier than thou assistant cook, who was a seceder and very strictly religious, refused to take the milk in on Saturdays and Sundays. She thought it was a sin for the milkman to be working on the Sabbath Day, so she flatly refused to accept milk at the weekends. But of course Sophia's uncle soon put a stop to that.

* Chaidh . . . artillery – I went with the officer from the artillery.

Sophia was most afraid when she was left alone at night, when the nurses would be off on the spree. So she would crawl out of bed and go over to the big rocking horse, climb onto it and rock and rock. All in the darkness. And she would imagine herself on the train again . . . when they lived in Cranford she used to run up to the station and watch the big steam train come roaring through the tunnel, smothering the bridge and herself and everything for miles around with thick, black smoke. And when the train passed on, and the smoke cleared she would see her father coming up the steps; usually she got a row, because it was naughty of her to come by herself to meet the train. And that's what it felt like lying there in her bed, sometimes pulling her hair out, sweating, feverish and clouds would come over her, a sort of blackness. I suppose she would be fainting really. And all the time she thought that she was on that bridge watching the steam train come puffing through.

Uncle Duncan was truly good, kind and noble to me. I wouldn't allow anybody, doctors or nurses, to put the poultices on my chest except him. When I was recovering he sent me with my mother to Rothesay, Isle of Bute, to recuperate. I remember being wheeled along the promenade in a basket chair and into the village, seeing all the shops, being exceedingly spoilt and demanding to have anything I fancied bought for me. Little bedroom slippers with bunny rabbits on and all sort of nonsense like that.

But one day the nurse almost cured me. I was demanding to have a bottle of Virol, a thick, malty laxative. She made me take the whole, big bottle of that stuff, and, my goodness, I never asked for another thing thereafter! The consequences were dire, or, should I say – diarrhoea. And while my father was in charge of transport of ammunition for the War we went on to Skye.

They were leaving Glasgow on their way by train. Sophia was extremely excited about going up to Skye again. She'd been kitted out with new clothes; while she was so long ill in bed, she had grown a couple of inches and nothing fitted her any more. So she felt she looked really smart. They all got into the carriage in Glasgow, a very wonderful carriage, nice upholstery and arm pieces sticking out on the seats – to climb on if you wanted to, to turn the heater, a wee knob at the back of the seats – which went from hot to medium to cold. A great idea, and there were antimacassars beautifully clean and white on the backs of the seats.

The journey as far as Inverness was really comfortable. And then they proceeded on to the Kyle of Lochalsh train, for Skye. They'd gone a couple of stations when a lady and a little boy joined the carriage. They sat opposite and the little boy was most obnoxious. He fiddled about with the long leather strap for opening and shutting the main window on the door. Sophia remembered her father saying that many of the Highland men used to cut those straps off the windows and take them home, to sharpen up their cut-throat razors. Next the boy started pulling faces at Sophia and waggling his ears, pinching his nose. His mother handed him some green grapes and he split them in half, tried fitting them inside his eyelids. Then he started saying that he was the Kaiser, and making horrible faces at Sophia. She got very cross with him indeed.

He was very naughty, so she said, 'You're not the Kaiser! I know what the Kaiser looks like because I've seen him in the newspapers – he's got a tin helmet, there's a spiky thing sticking on the top of it. And he's not a bit like you!'

With that the boy's mother said, 'Behave yourself!' And she extracted a four-inch long pin from her hat and threatened him, said if he didn't behave himself he'd get a poke with that in his posterior. I think that really frightened him; he behaved himself for the rest of the journey.

They were handed in a luncheon basket at Strathcarron, a chicken, and a hotchpotch of tea, cups and saucers, bits of cake and it was very welcome. But the further north they got the worse the weather became. The mountains were clouded, the trees black, ominous and being torn by gusts of heavy wind; when they got to Kyle of Lochalsh they were told that the ferry would not be able to run, they would have to get on to a steamer and be dropped off at Broadford Pier. There they were met by a gig, horse-drawn, which would take them to Sophia's grandmother's house, and that was in Breakish.

Sophia didn't like it very much, there was a feel about it . . . she would get very easily tired, completely exhausted, and hallucinated sometimes. She could picture people about the house, and was sure somebody was in her bedroom. She didn't get to sleep very easily. And one night she woke up in the night screaming her heart out. Lizzie, one of the Highland maids, came to her rescue. Sophia told her, 'A lady all dressed in white had opened her bedroom door, walked in with her arms extended and was going to try to lift her out of the bed; so she'd smothered herself in the blankets and quilt, and simply screamed and screamed.' She was in such a terrible state they wrapped her in a rug and took her downstairs; her mother was so upset she had to send a messenger for the doctor in Broadford.

So Sophia's younger uncle, Jimmy, got on his horse and rode up to Broadford to see if he could get the doctor. The doctor very kindly in the middle of the night got on his horse, and they rode back together to Breakish to see what was wrong with Sophia. The doctor said that she'd had a very serious shock and was to stay in bed for a couple of days.

When he'd gone her mother asked her brother what Sophia had seen, what did he think?'

And he said, 'Well, it's very feasible that she saw the Bride of Kilbride.'

'Who's that?' said her mother.

'Well, she's been seen quite frequently in these parts. She's a poor woman who had been deserted on her wedding night by one of the MacKinnon chieftains. He had left her, abandoned her completely and she was with child. However, she lost her child and she herself died soon afterwards. They do say that when a very sick child is about to die she will appear with outstretched arms and try and lift the child from its cot, its cradle or its bed.' Whether it's true or not, heaven only knows. But Uncle Jimmy firmly believed it.

At that time all the young men in Breakish were being called up for World War I. We would be having breakfast on the old wooden table and these handsome young sons of Rebecca's, my uncles, would be sitting in a row on the trust or the bench against the wall eating their porridge. As a little girl of four I would be putting my arms round perhaps Uncle John for a while, pestering him and then, perhaps, moving along, putting my arms round and giving a kiss to Uncle Dan . . . and then the gig would arrive and the men in their kilts and their sporrans would be winding their puttees (uniform bandages) round their ankles. Perhaps one of them would have a little brass object in their sporran, rather like a comb with a split up the middle, into which he would squeeze the buttons of his uniform and polish them with brass cleaner.

And then there would be many tears and grandma, mother and Auntie Chrissie and all the grown-ups would hug each other and big tins – like Carr's Biscuit tins – would be filled with sandwiches and flasks would be filled. Bottles would be hidden in various overcoat pockets and the gig, a kind of coach, was brought out and there would be four horses harnessed. All the men would clamber on board and wave and shout. Tears would be flowing and off they would go, to be sent out to Flanders or some such place to be killed. Almost every house in Breakish gave up its young men (see plate 14).

They were all very smart in their kilts and their immaculately clean putties, the regalia that Highland soldiers look so fascinating in. But the terrible tragedy was only a few of them ever came back home again. And Sophia's grandmother lost three of her sons in that terrible World War I, still going on. One night she had a dream that one of her sons was coming home and that she would have to get up and prepare for his arrival. She went to a kist to fetch out the blankets. It was full of Highland woollen blankets and in the darkness, though she had a candle (there was no electricity in those days) she opened the lid and pulled one out. In the darkness she felt it over, and to her amazement she felt buttons on it, army buttons, brass ones that the men used to polish diligently on their uniforms. She was horrified and dropped the blanket, or coat, as it now was, and in the morning she got her older son to look in the chest and see if the uniform coat was in there. It was not of course.

And the next thing was they got one of these dreaded telegrams to say that he was missing, presumed dead. So that's the sort of thing that made the stay in Breakish a very sad one.

But the village was really a very interesting place, and my grandmother's house was right in the centre of the action. Sometimes after a cattle sale the older men would get very plastered. They'd whip off their jackets and start wrestling at the back of the house. This was very exciting to watch. I always rather enjoyed a fight. It wasn't unknown either to set the cockerels at each other. I know this is an illegal sport nowadays, but it wasn't unknown in parts of Skye. Not that they would bet on the winning cockerel and not that they would let it go to extremes: they didn't allow the cockerels to destroy each other, but thoroughly enjoyed watching them attack.

All the washing was done down at the lower end of the Entry Mór in the river. Blankets, sheets, chemises and long johns, stockings, long red flannel skirts, black silk skirts, all kind of clothes were taken down to the dyke that ran along the edge of the river. A big fire would be built, a huge cauldron put on the fire and the clothes boiled, those that you could boil. And then the women would sit along the edge of the river with a scrubbing brush, a big hunk of carbolic soap and start scrubbing, scrubbing and bashing the clothes like they do in France on rocks and stones. There were big beautiful stepping-stones across that river. I used to love jumping from one to the other.

Aunt Belle, Uncle Duncan's wife, was very keen on hygiene.

She used to collect all the children. Having a big bag with sponges, soaps, combs and what they called 'dust combs', she would take the children down to this self-same river, rub paraffin into their heads and comb their hair until she got the choked nits and lice out in handfuls onto her little dust comb. Then she would wash their hair in the river until it was squeaky-clean. The ironing was done in the house. They used to heat two big irons on the burning hot range, then get a cloth, get hold of the handles, turn them upside down and spit on them. If the spit sizzled, then it was ready to be used to iron the clothes on the kitchen table. I remember my beautiful mother doing this job one day.

She had just spat on the iron and was taking it over to the table when a horrid little man came in and started being over familiar with her, and tormenting her. So she got hold of the iron and chased him right out of the house, right down the croft with this burning hot iron! We never saw him again.

Of an evening my Uncle Jimmy, Seumas an Taillear, would tell me wonderful stories. I always remember one – it was about two little twins, very young babies really, and they had wandered off and had gone across the river . . .

It starts with Eachan out on the croft leaning against the old stone dyke. He was half drunk, of course, if not more than half, and lazily gazing at a wretched sheep, its wool all trailing on the ground covered with muck. And a beautiful bird came fluttering down and alighted on the sheep's backside, started hunting for ticks or lice or some such thing. It would certainly get a good meal because Eachan's sheep were totally neglected. They'd not been dipped and they'd not been sheared. In fact he was a useless rascal. He'd been married for three years to a lovely girl. Her name was Annag and she was back in the house busily trying to do some ironing for her little twin daughters. There was a big old iron range with a good fire in it in the kitchen, and she was heating a couple of old-fashioned irons; electricity had not reached this island and wouldn't for many years to come.

So she lifted one with a cloth round its handle, turned it up and spat on it. It sizzled; so she would then wipe the iron on a folded piece of brown paper to clean it and proceed to iron the clothes on an old folded blanket on the kitchen table. This she was doing when her husband Eachan lurched through the door. Swearing at the dog and kicking it out of the house, he came straight up to her.

He shoved the blanket and the clothes aside, gave her a thump on her shoulder and said, 'What are you doing that for? Why haven't you got my dinner ready?'

And she said, 'Well, Eachan, you've just had your dinner, I gave it to you half an hour ago.'

'Liar,' he said and started clobbering her. Accidentally the iron she was holding twisted, he pushed her again and the iron burnt her wrists. With the agony and pain of it she almost collapsed on the floor.

This was enough. She'd lived with this brute for three years now and she couldn't stand any more of it. Since the children were out playing she decided to run to the next croft where her father and her brothers lived. She would tell them of the abuse she was getting, tell them that time had come now, she could really live with him no longer.

And for once her father and her brothers agreed with her. Things were going too far altogether. The poor girl had suffered terrible abuse and everybody in the village was heart sorry for her. The men for some time now had been getting together and trying to decide what to do about it. So, today Geordie and her father took the matter into their own hands.

It was bad weather, mind you, the snow was thick, it was November. So they thought they would try an old-fashioned punishment, they would tar and feather him and roll him in the snow. That's what used to be done with blaggarts like that. So they looked around for some rope that they cut off a fishing net. Then they looked for some tar but there wasn't any handy or any left, so they decided to use black treacle instead. And together with three more of Annag's brothers they marched down to Annag's croft, grabbed a hold of the fellow screaming and yelling as he was. They smeared him with treacle and feathers (from a torn pillow), tied him in the fishnet ropes and hauled him down to the shore, flung him into a rowing boat.

They then rowed him out to the middle of the Sound of Raasay where there was a buoy floating. They tied him to the buoy, gagged him, left him there and rowed back home.

Now the strange thing is that the Almighty has some very odd ways . . . it's not always the good that He helps. He sometimes helps those we would consider not worth helping. It quite often happens. And so it happened that the seagulls, when they realised the ropes that Eachan was tied with were smothered in fish oil, and they rather fancied the taste of the treacle, and they started to peck at him. And they pecked, pecked and pecked so much at the ropes that Eachan was able to struggle and loose himself: whether by good fortune or bad, there happened to be a naval cruiser passing by which had on board the press-gang. In those day (round about the Napoleonic Wars) the press-gang would pick up any men they could lay their hands on and use them in the war, either as sailors or as soldiers depending on where they were sailing to.

They rescued Eachan, pulled him on board the ship and eventually many months later he landed in Canada. We know that because he'd written to his parents. He'd written to tell them that he'd escaped from the ship in Vancouver and found his way up to the Yukon where he got employment rolling huge full-length logs down the river. He worked at that for some time, then got a job employed on a building site. He worked there for some months when he had a terrible accident. He was wearing sandshoes with rubber soles, and the scaffolding was wet. It had been raining, he slid and fell to his death.

Now the astonishing thing was he was entitled to compensation, a considerable amount of money. And they wrote to Annag from Canada, told her that they were returning the body to his home. One day a big shiny elaborate coffin arrived with brass handles and all, and the people all clustered round. When they opened the lid they were astonished. There was Eachan who had always been a terrible-looking tramp, but now he was dressed in an immaculate blue suit, a bow tie and shiny patent leather shoes – looking quite the toff. They couldn't believe their eyes. Needless to say the funeral was a great success. Everyone turned up for miles around. It was more like a wedding than a funeral and the little twins were immaculately dressed in new pink silk dresses with seed pearl embroidery on them.

It took some time for Annag to adjust herself to being a widow and her sisters-in-law, her father and brothers all insisted that she go and live with them for a while. So she packed up and took the twins, went to live in the next croft. But she was very listless and felt inadequate. She wanted to do everything she could to help the household keep going and she was very good at cooking and baking. She thought her best plan was to help in that direction.

She used to make bannocks and oatcakes, what they call aran coirc in the Gaelic. They were the size of dinner plates, very thick, and placed between a stirret, two wire mesh containers in front of the fire on the old grate until they roasted brown on each side. Then they were removed from the fire and put on a tea cloth on the dresser or the table. And she used to bake in this way daily; or, sometimes she would go to the field, help bring in the corn or whatever the season demanded.

She would take buttermilk and her oatcakes down for the men and the women who were working. After a while she adjusted herself and was very popular in the whole community. And the twins were very happy. When she worked in the field there was a cousin who looked after the twins when she was out. Not very bright; she was called Flora, was quite young and a bit irresponsible. But she loved the twins and stood by them while Annag was out working in the field.

Once or twice a year a travelling van used to come round with an Indian who'd been in the Highlands for many years, a well-respected man. He had a wonderful stock of clothes, brooches, books and everything you could think of. It was a great excitement when he'd come around the villages. People used to flock down to his van and select long johns for their husbands and semmits for their children. And this was too much for Flora one day.

When she heard the van coming she left the back door open and ran down to the van, couldn't resist it. She was there for some time, examining all the clothes, the stockings and everything, and forgot all about the twins. They must have decided to run outside to play and the awful thing was – they completely disappeared. When Flora came back to look for them she couldn't find them anywhere! She alerted the people in the field and everybody went looking for the twins. But they could not find them anywhere. Annag was in tears, hysterical, screaming and fainting, in a terrible state. In such a bad state that the women decided they must get her back into the house, get some tea into her, try to calm her down, give her a wee dram or something to steady her.

They did this and then left her there for a while to rest, to weep and to be alone with her thoughts while they proceeded to look for the children. All the men were out looking everywhere they could think of and there was no sign of them. Meanwhile, Annag was huddled up in an old armchair weeping her eyes out silently, when suddenly in came Eachan's dirty old collie dog. Silently the collie dog moved towards the old iron range, and very cleverly dragged the oatcake out of its cage, carried it in its mouth, then made for the door with it. Now Annag was too distressed and too stunned. And the dog didn't see her or had ignored her.

So Annag tried to pull herself together, and thought, 'Why would he do that? Where is he going with that?' And she got up, followed the dog outside. She could see him going down the croft. She followed him. He went in the direction of an old fox's lair; there had been a fox, but Eachan had shot it a while back. So the lair was deserted except for a few feathers and bones left from the chickens that the fox had stolen from her henhouse.

Over and above that there'd been some very bad weather, some strong winds, and there'd been a landfall, the earth had fallen in over the top of the fox's lair. Almost the whole of it was covered in earth, the ground had receded and there was a big hole. And when Annag got there she saw the dog go down, into the hole. She wouldn't fit into it, or any grown-up human being, but the dog manoeuvred its way down. Then she heard the sound of her children's voices. They were crying and shouting, and obviously the dog was feeding them, or giving them the oatcake that she'd made and he had stolen, from in front of the fire. It was a miracle. She couldn't get down the hole herself but she stood up, yelled and yelled till they heard her.

Her brothers came running. They got shovels and dug the hole bigger and were able eventually to get the children out. It was a miracle! And Annag drew her children to her bosoms and took them back home. The dog was brought in, made a great fuss of and in due time it was bathed, cleaned, combed, and brushed – this dirty old dog of Eachan's was a superb-looking animal! They'd bought him a beautiful collar and decided to give him a name; he had never had one before, was always kicked out of the house and told, 'Thalla mach a seo!' (which means, get out of here). But now they decided to give him a real name – Hero – they thought this was most suitable for such a brave and intelligent dog.

And Annag, now contented of an evening, would rock her children to sleep singing a little ditty in Gaelic; it's a very old one and was called 'Oran na Sean Mhaighdean' (which means, the old maid's song). And she would sing:

> Ged a bhithe' e crùbach crom
> Ged a bhithe' e dubh no donn
> B'fhearr leam gun tigeadh e

(which means, whether he is black or brown, whether he is bent or lame I would rather that he would come to me). And perhaps she would someday meet a man who would give her the comforts and love that she well deserves.

They found the two little twins surrounded by lumps of oatcake, which they were trying to chew, and the dog was guarding them. It used to bring tears to my eyes; they were still alive, and it happens to be a true story believe it or not.

My Uncle Jimmy would tell funny stories as well as sad ones while he sat in his big, high-backed chair attending to his boots, scraping the mud off them first, wiping them over and then putting large amounts of dubbin well into the leather, preparing them for the next time he would be out on the hill.

He told of an old bodach who was extremely religious, a very good man: he would say his prayers many times a day and go out late at night, sometimes on dark nights, sometimes in the moonlight.

He would kneel down beside the dyke and pray at great length. So the young lads thought they would take the mickey out of him and would squat down behind the dyke on the other side, start pelting him with peats. And he would be heard to jump up and shout, 'O Dhia, nach tuíg thu fun idir?' (O God, do you not understand fun at all?)

And there were many other stories he told, mainly in Gaelic.

Of an evening Duncan MacPherson, Uncle Jimmy's post-man, would come in and add to the stories, and, by golly, they were good ones, because he'd served in the army during World War I. His stories were just magnificent, and so were the medals and other paraphernalia he had hanging on his wall at home. He had a daughter Mary, and she was my very good friend. We used to play with each other down on the croft and on sunny days we would gather lots of daisies and make magnificent daisy chains. Sometimes I would take my beloved rag book down and share it with her. I shared a lot of my life with her, because when she grew up she became a secretary in the Gaelic Department of the BBC in Glasgow, and I saw quite a bit of her then.

Cranford

After spending the summer months on Skye, my mother would take my brothers and myself back down south to be with my father in Cranford for the winter (see plate 1). As a child it was sad leaving Skye: I could no longer visit the Balbhan and the MacKintoshes, the Robertsons and all my friends; no longer stand and admire the beautiful mud floor in the MacKintoshes' house, the little built-in bed tucked into the wall and curtained off – all these quaint things I felt I would probably never see again. I would play in the ditches and the clay pit up by the old hut where they used to thresh corn or down by the well. But in the summer again we would return.

On Skye Uncle Duncan had become very prosperous, and took Kinloch Lodge for the shooting (see plate 11). He asked my mother to look after it while he was away and use it until he was ready to go north himself with his family (he lived in Glasgow). So there we were, fortunately, with free travelling on all the British Railways; we stayed part of the time on the farm and the rest of the time in the big house, Kinloch Lodge. Uncle Duncan had given the farm to my mother's sister, Chrissie, who was at that time living in Glasgow and had four children. They all moved up to Skye to run the farm, and that's how we would join up with the children, our lot and their lot, and all stravaig off over the moorland to Drumfearn School.

I used to be sent off to school, not to learn anything, but just to sit there – because I had been so ill. I was given bits of coloured paper and a little scent bottle with a rubber attachment you squeezed, water would come out of it to clean your slate. If the schoolchildren were late by any chance they would be very severely reprimanded by the schoolmaster, but this never happened to me, fortunately.

Uncle Duncan had by this time a yacht called *The Trident*, with five of a crew and a skipper from Breakish called Gillespie Uilleam (see plate 5). We were all allowed to come on board and would often sail to Mallaig, to meet the train with Uncle Duncan on it. I remember I was always very impressed with this dapper little uncle of mine, his bowler hat, rolled umbrella and immaculate suit coming off the train at Mallaig; and we would all sail back to Kinloch. But it was no time at all before he was changed into his rough tweed jacket and his kilt, looking every inch a Hielan' laird.

Now my mother was pregnant again, having lost a baby earlier on in Breakish. I found this awfully sad. And in order to be quite sure that she would have the next baby safely, we all travelled back to Liverpool so that she could stay with Nurse Tinkler, the midwife who had brought myself and my brothers into the world.

And that's how my sister Morag was born in a little house in Liverpool; it wasn't big enough for my brothers and myself, so I was sent over to New Brighton to stay with my father's sister-in-law, and the two boys were sent to a place called Hailbank to live with my father's one and only sister.

When Morag was born I returned, and spent much of my time with my mother in Nurse Tinkler's house. Nurse Tinkler's husband was away at sea; in fact he was on the *Lusitania*, and while I was there the big ship was sunk and Mr Tinkler saved two of the little boys whose parents had drowned, so he brought them home and adopted them. He had them living in the house with his wife. He was a very kind man – this is just the sort of thing he would do. There was a cellar in the house, and being a ship's carpenter and engineer he would spend much of his time in there making, believe it or not, an enormous doll's house for me – one that I could walk in and out of. I used to play in their small garden on the swing – I was sure if I swung hard enough I would get right up to heaven, but this didn't happen – as yet!

So the day my sister Morag was born a little dove flew in at the window; I always remind my sister of this because it was surely to God a very, very good omen. They tried to send me to school in Liverpool, but it only lasted one day. And then my father was able to buy a house in Hoylake in Cheshire, and we all moved there. And that's where, a year or so later, my younger sister Cairistiona June was born.

Sophia Maria's father wanted his family with him in Hoylake, and so they left Skye for a few continuous years after the War finished. On their journey south they spent a couple of nights in Perth, in an enormous hotel that practically sat on top of the station. It belonged to a Highland man who had been at school with Sophia's mother and obviously adored her. So, kitting the babe for the sake of the nurse, as the saying goes, he would take Sophia to the shops and buy her anything she fancied. The day before they left to go further south, he took her into a jeweller's shop and bought her a watch. It was fascinating, oval-shaped with diamante all round it and blue enamelling. Very pretty and it actually worked, Sophia adored it. She swung her wrist about so that everybody in the hotel could see it.

The new Hoylake house was much to Sophia's liking. It was close to the sea just facing the promenade, which had a railing along it, wonderful for doing turn-ups and swinging on. Along at the end of the promenade there was a pavilion with pierrots in it, people who acted, sang and danced, and you were supposed to pay sixpence to get in to see them. But in the case of Sophia that wasn't necessary; she had very long, very thin legs and she could easily climb the barricade and find herself a seat without being noticed. So she developed a great love for all things theatrical. And she got a chance to do a bit of practising down on the shore, where the children all played around a black man with a banjo; he played, sang and entertained the people who came across from Liverpool, usually in summer. He would ask Sophia and other little girls and boys to dance to his music; they did willingly because Sophia was a bit of a show-off. Sophia noticed after a time he wasn't a black man at all: he had stuff on his face and his hands that made him look black, but one hot day he threw off his boots and his feet were as white as white could be! So, he must have been an actor too.

Then there would be the fishermen down on the beach with their bare feet and their barrows, full of flukes and flounders they'd been catching. Sometimes they would give Sophia a few, but more often than not they wanted some money for them. Of course she never had much in the way of pennies or sixpences to spend. In the mornings she would make her way down to the seashore, make sandcastles and play around, paddling and sometimes swimming. On a very low tide she could walk across to Hillbury Island, and with her father take a picnic.

At the other end of the promenade there was a small lighthouse that had been converted into a cinema, a very early one. The people who lived round about here didn't call it a lighthouse, they called it a 'beacon' which set

Sophia off in uncontrollable laughter. Because, after all, she had learned quite a bit of Gaelic when she stayed in Skye, and the word 'beucan' means the naughty parts of a man or a boy! The women used to hold their babies out, their boys, in front of the fire and chant in Gaelic,

> Tha beucan aig a'gille bheag
> Tha beucan aig a'gille bheag!
> (the little boy's got a beacon)

Then they would direct this 'thing' towards the fire and the baby was encouraged to pee on the peats so he would grow up with a good sense of direction. One can see why Sophia thought it was so hilariously funny.

She was privileged one night to go with her mother and father to watch a film. She hadn't seen a film before. Unfortunately this one was called *Ecce Homo*. It was very disturbing, about Jesus being persecuted and the Crown of Thorns being put on Him, all the horrible things that were done to Him, hanging Him on the cross, everything. All this was far too much for Sophia, she was in floods of tears and very upset, so they got her out and started walking home along the promenade when she totally collapsed. Her father carried her home, they sent for the doctor and he said, like the doctor in Skye, that it had been too frightening for her, she'd made herself ill emotionally: 'She must rest and keep quiet for a couple of days.'

So there she was in bed being looked after by the Highland maid her mother had brought with her from Skye and by her own mother. The maid was asked to bring a basin so that Sophia could have a bed wash.

Instead of bringing an ordinary basin, I'm afraid this particular maid was a bit odd: she brought an immaculately clean chamber pot with hot water, scented soap and talcum powder. Sophia's mother just accepted this and washed Sophia down; and it was so, so soothing and refreshing Sophia thought it was a very good idea, much better than trying to use the big ewer and basin popular in those days.

The highly sensitive and imaginative girl was advised to take daily walks along the seashore to try and regain her health. This suited Sophia very well, because she was able to dream, tell herself stories and admire the beautiful sunset in the late afternoons, the sunset that Turner had painted so beautifully. Sophia wished she could paint, she would love to have a go at depicting these wonderful sunsets. She also loved listening to the great big ships on the horizon making their way along the Mersey to strange foreign parts. She felt she would like to get on one of them and sail far, far away to somewhere like Fiji, wear a raffia skirt, and she could teach the girls to dance the Charleston. She'd just managed to learn to it herself.

Her mother had taken her up to London to stay for a few days with some cousins, and they taught Sophia how to do the dance. They also took her to the theatre to hear Paul Robeson singing 'Old Man River' so superbly. She was taken all round London, the wonderful buildings and museums; her mother also took her to Old Bond Street, got her a new dress and a lovely pair of new shoes in a shop called Pinnes. She was very, very proud of these shoes! And when she got home kept them carefully, only wearing them on special occasions, because they did nip a bit.

One day back home she was walking along the sands with her father, still very frail and delicate-looking, and they met an eccentric old man who was an acquaintance of her father's. His shoelaces were undone, he was wearing a bowtie and his hair was all over the place. He stopped in front of Sophia and stared at her. Then he said to her father, 'Would you mind very much if I painted a portrait of your daughter?'

And her father said, 'Well, I suppose that would be really rather nice, but I don't know if I can afford it.' He knew this man was an eminent painter, Frank T Copnall, who lived in Hoylake. And so her father was really rather flattered.

Since Sophia didn't go to school at all, it was arranged she would go through to Liverpool each day with her father when he went to work. Copnall had a studio there, a huge studio. Sophia was made to sit for hours, placed on a very high dais or two or three boxes and a chair, while he ran about getting a good look at her from various angles and dashing back to his canvas to put down what he had seen, quite extraordinary. He would run to the far end of his studio, then run back again and quickly daub paint onto his canvas, run away again and then back again; he kept on doing this till he was quite out of breath and very excited.

Meanwhile, after hours and hours of sitting in this way, Sophia needed to spend a penny and there was no way she could stop him on his marathon racing to tell him such a thing. However, a little old woman called Mrs Jones used to come in daily to clean his paint brushes, and when he wasn't looking Sophia managed to draw her attention. She was very deaf, it was difficult to catch her attention and Sophia whispered to her that

she badly needed to pee. Mrs Jones understood immediately, and oh, dear me, what a relief that was!

Sometimes Copnall and her father would go off,
leaving Sophia with the caretaker when they went for
a pint of beer; they'd take rather a long time before they
got back. During this period Sophia would rake amongst
the numerous canvases, there were piles all round the
studio. She loved examining them, thinking how much
she would love to be able to paint like that herself.

One day she stumbled over an old, decrepit-looking,
huge canvas that was very frightening, really. It depicted
a graveyard with human beings rising from the graves,
sitting on these gravestones and raising their arms in the
air, all different people. But one face struck her forcibly
in that it was extremely ugly – the man had a scar down
the side of his face with blood dripping – it was frightening. And Sophia thought she was going to have a dizzy
turn again. The face of the man halfway out of the grave
disturbed her so much that she didn't forget it for a very
long time.

Through time she was gradually getting stronger and
sleeping better, although she did have a recurring dream,
not unpleasant. It was of a lady, tall, slender, beautiful,
emerging from a train and obscured by the smoke from
the engine, just as her father had been in the long gone
days in Cranford. This lady had a beautiful face, most
extraordinary features, her nostrils like tiny little shells
that shimmered, and she had the prettiest mouth. In the
dream she would say to Sophia, 'Don't be afraid, you
may find it difficult to cope with your next adventure,
but don't be frightened, be strong! Because everything
will be all right. Mark my words, you will be safe!' And
she would shimmer away behind the smoke again.

Sophia wondered what it all meant. She would lie awake for hours listening to the foghorns blasting out and moaning and groaning from the big ships in the Mersey and often get up feeling still tired, but the best thing for her was to walk on the shore beside the sea, and she did this now daily.

One very cold, very dull day at the end of winter, she took rather a long walk along the sands for about half a mile, and then decided to turn, return home. As she did so she saw a man come leaping out from the sand-hills; their tops were overgrown with grasses, like heaps, some larger than others, and the man came leaping through the sand-hills, down one minute and up the next – then to her horror came running towards her! He came right up to her, got a hold of her arm, twisted it painfully and with some sort of screwdriver or sharp pin he managed to rip her lovely little watch off her wrist, and also take her handbag. She couldn't scream, she couldn't do anything, she was absolutely frozen and completely terrified. And then, she realised she'd seen this fellow before: it was the ugly man in the painting in Mr Copnall's studio, even down to the scar on the side of his face! It was him all right – she was more petrified than ever. It was no use screaming, there was nobody about, not a single soul. And in case he was going to slit her throat or in some way kill her, she turned on her heel and dashed for the sea. She ran right out into the sea, her clothes were weighed down with the water, but she managed to get far enough out to be sure she would not be pursued. He was such a wretched-looking creature, as though water had never touched him in his life and she didn't think it likely that he would come after her in the sea. She realised that he was a common thief, if she stayed out there in the perishing sea for a little while longer he would go back the way that he had come. And this he did. He ran off, throwing her handbag into the sea, having emptied it of any money, and, of course, he had her beloved little watch. He disappeared amongst the sand-hills, up one, down another, zigzagging about until he disappeared completely.

She got ashore, shook herself off – there was no question of being able to dry herself – and started to run and run, run and run, until she at long last fell into her front door, and shouted for her mother who put her into a hot bath and even gave her a tiny sip of brandy while her father contacted the police. They were not very long in coming. Meanwhile, Sophia feeling much refreshed and very excited, fished out her best dress and the pretty shoes that had been bought in Bond Street, preened herself in front of the long mirror, even pinched a touch of her mother's make-up. She sauntered down the staircase kicking her young brothers aside, as they were all agog – nothing like this had happened in the home ever – made her way into the dining room. The police had already arrived, and they put three huge volumes of photographs on the dining room table. But there was still room for Sophia to heave herself onto the corner of the table and swing her silk-stockinged legs, twisting her ankles hither and thither so that the younger of the policemen could not fail to see her attractive new shoes!

It took ages and ages to go through the photographs of criminals, villains of every description. Sophia diligently looked carefully at each and every face. But she couldn't see the face of that terrifying man. Photograph after photograph the police kept saying, 'Is that him? Is that him?'

And Sophia would shake her head and say, 'No, no, I'm sure it's not.' Till she started to get sleepy and bored, and was bored stiff by the time they got through two of the big volumes of photographs. It wasn't until they'd started on the third one that she said in an excited shout, 'Stop, stop! That's him, that's him!'

And there he was, the ugly, the evil-looking fellow with a scar down the side of his face. So she was able to tell them in full detail about the studio in Liverpool, Mr Copnall the artist and how she had come across this big old painting.

This information was very useful to the police; they lost no time in contacting Copnall and he was very helpful too. He said that he had engaged this ugly-looking fellow because he wanted to put an evil character into his painting. It was just a piece of luck that he'd walked along the road, saw this ugly-looking creature with a barrow heaped with old clothes, shoes and books and things. Evidently, he was a rag-and-bone man to trade and this was very handy for him, because he was able to have access to all the houses round about Liverpool. He cleared them, knew their layout, it was easy to burgle them at night. Eventually he got a sentence from the judge of three years in prison.

Frank T Copnall made three paintings of me (alias Sophia) and one of them was hung in The Paris Salon and one hung in The London Gallery (see plate 23). He then decided to paint my mother who had popped in frequently to see how he was getting on. She was a very good-looking lady. Then when Uncle Duncan saw these portraits, he decided to commission Copnall to do one of Ruby and one of Màiri (my cousins), and so it went on.

My father would take me with him often, show me the sights of Liverpool, the Cathedral, the museums and everywhere, tell me about the liver birds, take me down to the landing stage. One day he showed me where the Negroes used to be chained and sold years before, within his memory, about 1890. He said he could still remember when these poor Negroes were chained to what looked like granite stools awaiting to be shipped to America. I thought it was terribly sad.

Our home in Hoylake was always open house to any Highlanders, particularly those coming from Skye, and every year flocks of people used to come down for the Grand National. My mother was very keen on horses, and so was my Uncle Duncan. He would bring his friends from Glasgow and from Perth, they would all very eagerly put their bets on the horses. Uncle Duncan took me when I was quite young to my first Grand National. I must have been very puny, skinny and lightweight, because in the crowd I couldn't see. So he put me on his shoulders with one leg dangling either side of his neck and I was able to see the race from that advantage.

He was also very liberal with his money with us kids, thought nothing of handing us a fiver each. I remember I did a terrible thing with mine one time: I sneaked off, went to the shops and bought five pounds' worth of Turkish delight. When I got back home I didn't know how to smuggle it out of sight, and it was quite a weighty parcel. So I undid it; and we had a steep staircase carpeted with brass stair rods. I put about four or five of the Turkish delights behind the carpet on the upturn of the stairs all the way up – on each step Turkish delight, Turkish delight, Turkish delight – right up to the top. And I would eat my way all the way down again. It took me about a year, and I was never sick.

As we were all growing up and my mother entertained a lot, she needed extra help. So she sent to a place called Bru Barvas in Stornoway, Isle of Lewis, for two girls. One was called Annie Finlayson and the other was her sister Màiri. They were brought down to be with us in Hoylake. Annie Finlayson was a great success and we all became very fond of her indeed but poor Màiri was terribly homesick from the moment she arrived until she departed. Father just had to pack her off back home because she did nothing but cry and cry.

Mother had a good friend called Mrs Rigby and her husband was very artistic. In fact, he owned a false teeth manufacturing establishment, and his wife came from New Zealand. He had met her when he was sent out there to carve the pews in Christchurch, South Island. He presented me with a necklace of his false teeth. Not his own, but the false teeth that he had made. He had them coloured, each tooth differently. I thought it was magnificent and enjoyed wearing them, but all the grown ups thought it was disgusting – you can never depend on people's taste – one man's meat is another man's poison.

Mother was a great one for buying and selling houses. She was a very good businesswoman and always made a profit. So, we packed up from the first house in Hoylake and went to live in West Kirby. The house she bought had belonged to Sir Thomas Carlyle's sister, who died of cancer. We weren't very comfortable in the house at all. Indeed, my father considered that it was haunted. He believed he saw the ghost of Thomas Carlyle's sister in his dressing room on more than one occasion.

So, mother sold that house and we all went to live in Arnott House, in Mells. And again she sold at a profit and we went to live in another house; she again sold at a profit and we went to live in another house, this time over on the other side of Liverpool in The Five Lamps, a house between Crosby and Waterloo. This was an enormous house and very difficult, hard to run. By now my father had come to retirement age. We all decided to go back to Skye and live in Liveras, Broadford. But just before we left Hoylake a very extraordinary thing happened: at the crack of dawn one Sunday morning there was a loud knocking at the door, my mother went down to find a couple of policemen standing there with two small raggedy boys.

The policeman said, 'Are you Mrs Christopher Sykes?'

Mother said, 'Yes.'

And they said, 'Do you know these boys?'

And mother said, 'Well, they seem familiar in a strange way.'

The policeman said, 'Well, they say they're looking for you!'

And the boys started to say, 'Oh please, please Mrs Sykes, will you take us in? Please, Mrs Sykes, we've run away from home.'

Then mother realised who they were – the two orphans who had been rescued by Mr Tinkler from the *Lusitania*, the boys he'd taken back to his wife to look after. Well, I'm sure Mrs Tinkler would have been very kind to them, really, but they thought otherwise and had walked all the way from Liverpool to Hoylake. Except of course there was no tunnel then, and they had to get on the Birkenhead ferry. I don't know how they made their way from there to the sand-hills in Hoylake. It had become dark, nightfall had come down, and they decided to bury themselves in the sand. Somebody had seen them and alerted the police. The police questioned them and they kept saying, 'We want to find Mrs Sykes, we want to live with Mrs Sykes.' So that's how they were brought to us.

Well, mother fed them and re-clothed them – their big toes were sticking out of their sand shoes, their noses were running, they were miserably hungry and she saw to them. Of course she couldn't possibly keep them because my sister June had been born and there were five of us; if she had kept them that would have been seven children, and my father didn't have a very big salary. So they had to be sent back to Mrs Tinkler. I never heard what happened to them after that.

So, on our way to Skye! My father arranged with the railways to take all our furniture up to Kyle of Lochalsh, then it was taken off the train by cranes and put onto the steamer that took it to Broadford Pier. Then onto cranes again and tossed over to the pier where Aonghas Mór the carrier, with his cart and his horse, took each bit of furniture, piece by piece to Liveras, including the lovely dining room suite mother had bought with the house that belonged to Thomas Carlyle's sister. At one time that furniture, which is still in the family, had been in his house in Chelsea, we are told.

So there we were settling into Liveras in Broadford. Amongst our stuff was a big scrub wood dresser with shelves my father kept full of books. I took a delight in climbing onto the dresser and starting, to try, to read – each book one after another – understanding hardly any of it. Whether it did any good or not I don't know, but it is really all the education I ever got. At that time I wrote an essay, my first bit of scribbling, sent it off and won a prize! The story was about Lady Pam and Thora, two Shetland ponies that used to drive the nursery cart at Skeabost. Before they could do that of course my cousins Catriona and Jack and I had had to break these ponies in, thrilling and exciting work. The lady mayoress in Birkenhead was to give me a prize for that story.

The house in Liveras was bought by my Uncle Duncan for his mother, and her brother Donald. The story is told how it was necessary for my mother to pack up all our trunks, wrap the babies up well and return to Skye for the christenings of each one of her children: Morag was christened in Kinloch and Cairistiona in Breakish.

One day, I was about eleven, mother and I were on *The Trident* and Uncle Duncan's guests that day were Mrs Kennedy Fraser and her daughter Patuffa. Sitting on deck on a beautiful sunny day sailing into Broadford Bay my mother remarked to my Uncle Duncan, pointing to a house near the pier, 'I do love that house, Liveras.'

And he said, 'Yes, it's nicely situated. I like it myself.' And he said to my mother, 'Would you like to have it, Mairianna?'

And she said, 'Oh, I would love to have it but I couldn't live in it, not while the children are at this young age and while Chris is still in Liverpool. But it would be lovely to have it, certainly.'

And Uncle Duncan said, 'I'll tell you what I'll do – I'll buy it and put mother in it.' And so he put my grandmother and a housekeeper, who was a distant relative called Katie, into the house that used to be occupied by the minister, Maighstir Lamont, who wrote a book about Strath in the Isle of Skye.

With five of us kids now in Liveras, I would spend much of my time in Kyleakin at Kyle Farm with my mother's sister, Auntie Chrissie, and my Uncle Farquhar and their large family, six of them. We had a whale of a time climbing the hills, working the fields, shearing the sheep. And Auntie Chrissie was a very enterprising lady. She heard of a business that was going to be sold in Mallaig. It was a factory that made aerated waters. We had no fizzy waters in Skye in those days, only uisge beathe (the water of life, whisky).

So Auntie Chrissie asked me if I'd like to accompany her on

the steamer to Mallaig, she would negotiate, find out if she could purchase this factory. And of course I was only too pleased! So we set off on the steamer, got to Mallaig where we had relations, had lunch with them and spent a very pleasant day. Auntie Chrissie went to see the factory and decided against it. So towards evening it was time to catch the steamer back home, to Broadford or Kyleakin.

We were a bit late, had spent a lot of time with friends and in shops. We rushed down to the pier to get on the steamer. Now it was a very low tide, and the names of the steamers didn't reach above the parapet. We were late already, the steamer was about to leave, so we jumped on board. There was a lovely smell of fresh herring being cooked, so we went below and ordered a high tea. We'd have just time to eat the herring until we would get into Broadford Pier.

We were enjoying our meal immensely, and Auntie Chrissie asked the waiter, 'When are we due in? It seems to be taking quite a while to get to Broadford.'

He said, 'We're not going to Broadford; we're going to North Uist.'

'What!' said Auntie Chrissie.

'Yes, we're going straight out to the Outer Isles.'

'Well, we, we can't go to the Outer Isles, we have to get off . . . how . . . what'll we do?'

He said, 'Well, you can't get off till tomorrow. We'll be coming back in the morning and then we can let you off at Broadford, round about lunch time.'

Well, you couldn't help seeing the funny side of it but we also felt rather squeamish. It was a rough crossing, late in the year and we were both very unhappy with mal de mer. We were very glad when, eventually, we got home to Broadford. Of course, both Auntie Chrissie's and my family were practically having a nervous breakdown; they had no way of knowing where we were or what had happened to us.

When I was in my early teens (1924) the lease expired on Kinloch so Uncle Duncan, to everyone's astonishment, bought Skeabost Estate in the north end of the island (see plate 12). He bought it from the MacDonalds of Tote. My older cousin Ruby, Uncle Duncan's daughter, had become engaged to Iain Hillary from Edinbane and a great wedding was planned at St Giles Cathedral in Edinburgh. Ruby's sister Catriona and I were small enough to be trainbearers (see plate 6). So we had to go south and get ourselves measured for Kate Greenaway dresses of silver lamellae with poke bonnets. We had a wonderful time. The bridesmaids were all beautifully dressed in green chiffon, and Ruby looked perfect. They went off for their honeymoon to France and Spain.

Every year I would be collected by Bain the chauffeur and driven to Skeabost to be with my cousins for the whole of the summer, sharing the same governesses and joining in all their activities. It was a wonderful life; we would sail round the island in *The Trident*, have dancing practices, play tennis (I was never allowed to play because of my heart condition), go fishing and have terrific times. We were very naughty sometimes and played pranks on people who might be staying. There was never a year without all kinds of interesting people coming to stay. Sometimes it would be Schiaparelli, the famous dress designer from America, because Uncle Duncan had a keen interest in tweed making. He'd converted some of the wood mills down at the quayside into workshops, placing looms in them and engaging people from the Outer Isles to weave the beautiful designs which Schiaparelli produced, creating a lighter type of tweed which was more marketable.

The summers in Skye seemed to be warmer. The climate seemed altogether better, everything was better; every summer up at the north end in Skeabost with my cousins – Uncle Duncan had six children and the youngest ones were twins, Catriona and Jack (about six months younger than me). We would swim in Loch Snizort off the end of the coal pier where the boat used to come in; the puffers, like the *Para Handy* which used to come in regularly and deliver the coal. So, it wasn't awfully clean and it wasn't awfully deep, but we used to plunge in there, swim and we had wonderful games. We couldn't drive a car, too young and we weren't invited to, so we would go up to the forest, and there was a broken-down tree, shape it in the form of a car front or a motor bicycle, make a saddle, sit on it and pretend that we were driving to all the magic places in the world. They were wonderful days.

One day we decided to camp out in the forest. So we acquired a lot of quilts, blankets and pillows and we raided the pantries, found all sorts of goodies, jellies, condensed milk, cinnamon sticks, tasty things, took them with us. We decided to stay all night in the forest. So when darkness came we snuggled down under our blankets and quilts. We were just beginning to get off to sleep in the middle of the night, in pitch darkness when a huge monster came into our tent and squatted down on our legs! We were absolutely terrified. Breathing hard and sharp and fast . . . not able to utter a word.

When suddenly a gentle voice said, 'It's all right, children, it's only me.'

And this was my Auntie Belle, Uncle Duncan's wife who'd got up herself in the middle of the night, worried about us I suppose, and she'd come down to be with us!

She spent the rest of the night in the tent. It was rather fun really.

And then sometimes Auntie Belle would come down herself and stay with us in Broadford. She came, as she said herself, for a complete rest, to be away from entertaining, visitors and people, all her commitments up in Skeabost. She would stay in bed for a very long time, right up till lunchtime. But she felt lonely and she really rather liked being entertained, someone to talk to. So she commandeered me to come and talk to her while she was in bed. I sat on a chair and asked her what she wanted me to talk about.

She said, 'All the gossip, darling, all the gossip!' So of course I didn't know an awful lot of gossip but what I did I told her about, and I always embellished it and made it sound much more exciting and dramatic than it really was. This pleased her enormously.

Now another of Uncle Duncan's children was Aloe. He was a darling, a bit older than me; I was very fond of him and he was very fond of me. And he could drive. He used to take the car and we would go off swimming, climbing, walking and enjoying each other's company.

One day we decided to go to Torrin, to the pool at the foot of Blàbheinn, the warm mountain. A huge pool is there with an enormous waterfall when the rains have been coming down. And there was a lot of rain lately. The river was in full spate, the waterfall magnificent. So I decided to have a swim. I didn't realise of course that Aloe had a camera in the car.

He went back for the camera. Meanwhile I stripped off almost to the buff and took a dive off a tall rock into the pool. Now I was no diver, it was very dangerous and I must have disappeared entirely. I swam around in the

pool and found that I could swim underneath the waterfall. When I got there I was astonished to find a big
passage, an alley that led into the darkness.

It was very, very dark, and I swam in the shallow water
halfway through. I could see the walls of this tunnel
glimmering with all kinds of lights, green ones, red ones,
blue ones and circles like small miniature rainbows going
round and round. And realising there was an opening at
the far end, I swam right out until I reached the open sea.
And I continued to swim. To my astonishment I came
upon a tiny island. Lo and behold, dotted here and there
were huge, big lions! They didn't seem to be fierce; they
seemed to be very quiet and passive, lying down. And then
a man came running towards me to the edge of the beach.

He said, 'Don't be afraid!'

I said, 'Well, aren't they fierce, won't they kill me,
won't they eat me?'

And he said, 'No, no, no, they won't, they never touch
any human flesh. They never touch flesh at all.' He said,
'We don't eat here. Come ashore!' And he stretched out
a long arm and hauled me onto the beach.

'How do you mean you don't eat?'

He said, 'Well, we don't need to eat.' He said, 'You
need to eat where you've come from, but we never need
to eat here. We refresh ourselves and regain energy
simply by going to sleep. We sleep for a long, long
time, then we waken refreshed and are able to get on
with our lives. We don't need food at all.' And he said,
'Come and see where I live.'

And I said, 'Well, yes . . .' And he took me more or
less up to the centre of the island where he had a sort of
cave. Inside it were all kinds of magnificent jewels, gold
and silver and diamonds. And he himself was wearing a

big cairngorm ring on the one hand and an amber ring on the other. He was exceedingly handsome, tall and blond with deep blue eyes. I couldn't make out exactly what he was wearing – strange garments which I had never seen before.

Although I was fascinated by him I felt somewhat afraid and he said, 'Don't be afraid of me, I'm sure we'll meet again. Perhaps not here, perhaps in some other place. We're bound to meet again.'

And I said, 'I must now swim back from whence I came.'

And he said, 'Well, don't go until you take this ring, and when you see me again we can exchange rings.'

I said, 'Oh, I can't do that!'

And he said, 'Oh yes, yes, you must! Take this ring.' So he put the cairngorm ring on my finger. And the next thing I knew, I'd come to . . . stretched on the bank above the Torrin pool, and Aloe was there . . . trying to resuscitate me.

He said, 'You know what's happened to you – you've got concussion! And you've got a bang on your head, it's bleeding badly. When you dived you must have banged into rocks on the bottom of the pool. I'll have to get you to hospital straightaway!' And he bundled me into the car, we motored through to the Broadford Hospital where I received five stitches on the side of my head.

Much later I discovered that Aloe had been taking photographs while I swam, he actually had one of me diving into the pool. The thing that annoyed me more than anything, he took these photographs when he went up to Cambridge, showed off about his girlfriend in Skye. I took umbrage and for some time didn't bother with that Aloe any more, changing my affections for Willie, the son of the manse in Broadford.

(Some twenty years later I met my tall, blond, blue-eyed man and we exchanged rings. Less than a month went by when we got married. And if that's not déjà vu I'll eat my hat!)

But by now I was aged sixteen, and the time came around for my cousin Catriona and myself to be allowed to go to the County Ball, an enormous thrill. It meant that we had to have quite a number of dresses, one for each of the practice nights which took place in the houses of friends – in Jock Mac-Donald's house in Viewfield, in Portree and in all the other VIP houses in Skye. People were invited to the house parties, and then went on from place to place, county to county.

There were all sorts of customs, you had to be very mannerly and well behaved. For instance, a lady could never walk from one room to another with the same cigarette. Before she left the one room she would have to stub it out then relight when she got to the next room. One went through a huge number of cigarettes and there would be an enormous amount of fag ends lying about, which I've no doubt would disappear in the morning. Those who could afford it would go from city to city where they would continue to have these magnificent occasions: Edinburgh, Perth. The Perth Ball was a very good one, and invariably they would end up in London. This was all very thrilling but hard going, because I didn't have an extensive wardrobe.

I couldn't write away for beautiful evening gowns, but a friend Mrs Pritchard, who used to come and stay with my mother in Liveras, volunteered to make some patterns.

Every year they have the so-called County Balls; the big houses invite people from far afield, London, America, all the countries in the world to Skye. Yachts, some very

luxurious, and boats of all kinds come for the balls to
Portree Bay. It's a wonderful sight at night seeing them
all glittering in the Bay. There's a lot of preparation
done: the old assembly hall has to be draped with plaids
and clumps of heather; and the officials get all the
goodies and all the catering sent up from London, from
Fortnam & Mason usually or Harvey Nichols or some
such place. The houses have practice nights when all the
incomers have to learn to do the eightsome reels
immaculately, the forty-twosomes and all the various
dances. And we girls are supposed to have about five
evening dresses, as lovely as they can be.

A very close friend, Mummy Pritch, stayed with us
regularly. She would get the material sent up and design
some dresses. I would carry the material and the patterns
down to Lower Breakish, a row of quaint fishermen's
houses at the edge of the sea. If the tide was out you
could get to one of these houses with dry feet. If the tide
was in you'd probably get soaked. However, there was a
little woman who did some beautiful sewing and lived in
one of these little houses.

She would have a peat fire. What fascinated me were
the crickets on the hearth chirping away. She was very
generous and would make me a lovely cup of tea with
some homemade pancakes, lashings of butter and jam
on them. It was quite an occasion to go down there.
Then I would give her Mummy Pritch's pattern and the
material, and she would run up dresses for me. And
believe it or not they were a great success, everybody
thought them wonderful.

Around this time Uncle Duncan decided to build a new house
in Breakish for my grandmother Rebecca and her brother

Donald, who was now a very old man. And so, although it was a tragedy, he had the old stone house pulled down, the thatch burnt and the trees sawn away. Of course, in order to get a water system into the house, the river was drained and the flagstones disappeared from the front of the house. All the magic had gone. But he had a very fine house built at great cost in its place, and so it was decided that grandma and Katie the housekeeper should go and live down there in Breakish with Grand-uncle Donald.

Sophia Maria was glad to know that her father had taken early retirement, and that World War I had finished. So her mother and herself, and indeed all of them were eager to get back to the Highlands. Sophia's father was looking forward to getting to Skye so that he could continue painting his landscapes. He was a very generous man and would give anything to his wife and his children, but for himself he wanted nothing. He would only allow himself a two and sixpenny tin paint box and two or three hairless brushes; with these he would struggle to do some quite good paintings in his time.

Sophia would accompany her father sometimes on his painting trips because she knew that the mountains would talk to her, they would talk back to her as they had to her ancestors before. By the age of twenty-one Sophia was grown up and much stronger. Her mother made her a clootie dumpling with a bunch of kitchen candles stuck on it, for her birthday and Uncle Neilag hired a car to bring her a sheep, a real sheep with a MacLeod tartan ribbon round its neck. But after eating up many of her mother's lupins, rhododendrons and catmint, the sheep disappeared, no doubt joining Neilag's flock nibbling the grass and basking on his nearby croft. Twenty-one and fancy-free! While the Skye mists deepened Sophia would dream of the billowing smoke – as the steam train came through Cranford Railway Bridge – all those years ago. Now World War II was pending. But like the train coming out of the tunnel, we hoped to come up to the light of the day (see plate 18).

The Theatrical Wren

I was beginning to get a bit restless at this time, had ambitions to go south and be a film star or some such thing. Staying so often at Skeabost had given me grandiose ideas, but I knew that if I left the island I was going to miss it all bitterly – the friends and interesting people I had met at Skeabost; the Governor of Uganda, MacKenzie King, would be staying there for a while. He had a crush on my cousin Màiri. And even Harry Lauder, whom they had made a great fuss of – guns were fired and bonfires lit on Caroline Hill. The servants were all lined up and Catriona and Jack and myself were allowed to come down in our nighties to listen to late night performances from that old genius. But it would all have to stop some day soon.

After the season I went back to Liveras. I knew I was getting impatient. One day I quarrelled with my father and said, 'Look, I want to go to London and I want to find a job. I'll go and stay with my brother Duncan.' He was now in London and employed by Uncle Duncan, he would find me digs, and I would see what I could do with my life. Strangely enough they agreed. That was when my life in London began.

Uncle Duncan had picked my brother Duncan to work in the whisky trade in London, because he was called after him. And I guessed that I might be able to get some accommodation from him. So I boarded the steamer which came regularly into the Broadford Pier every morning, sailed across with many dolphins following in the wake of the ship to the Kyle of

Lochalsh, then boarded the train to find that I was being accompanied by a fellow called Tom Peel – it was his brother I had been interested in. The whole family used to stay at the Broadford Hotel every summer, quite a large family, a girl and several boys. The only boy I really fancied was Gerald, the oldest one.

So I travelled with Tom and began to get a bit hungry, as one always did on the Highland Railway. Fortunately there was a pullman car and we could have lunch. I was rather disgusted that Tom didn't offer to pay for mine, I'd never had to pay for my own lunch in my life before. It was more offensive, because I was a vegetarian by now, and when I told the waiter to bring me a vegetable dish he brought me a plate full of gravy with two potatoes. Over and above that there was an old cailleach from Breakish whom I knew well sitting in the next seat wearing an ex-Army overcoat, full-length with buttons and a big trilby hat with hatpins. She kept on taking her fork, pushing her hat back to scratch her head with it, then continued to eat her meal. I was mortified!

But it was good to have the dining cars on the Highland Railway; prior to that picnic hampers had been handed in at Dingwall, and they were a lot of fun. I remember as a small child playing with a teapot on the floor of the compartment, and my brothers all squabbling for the various bits of china. There used to be a large chicken in a napkin, and anything you wanted really; if you telephoned or communicated in advance, everything was brought to your carriage – those were the days!

Of course there were hazards. Often we would be snowed up; all the men would have to get out of the train, be given shovels and have to shovel snow off the line – I remember my father doing that. But now, today with Tom Peel, it was all very satisfactory. A good many Sgitheanaichs had descended on London at that time. The Robertson family had bought a lovely house out in New Barnet and my cousin Ruby, who had married Iain Hillary from Edinbane, had a most beautiful house in Buckinghamshire down by the river. It had curly chimneys, Jacobean, and I often stayed there at weekends.

One year I did stay with my brother Duncan in London, and was able to go to the Ball in the Dorchester Hotel. I didn't have much money and I'd decided I was going to be a film star, go round all the agents and try to get myself into films. I wasn't having much luck. I did get one, though. It was a very early film with Douglas Fairbanks Junior down in the Denham Studios. My part was to be a dancing partner, and I'd danced all day from crack of dawn till the evening. Then I went to the Dorchester to the balls and danced all night! So, although immensely enjoyable, it was exhausting.

Sometimes there were Highland dances in Ballsover Street. One night I went to one and a lot of girls from Lewis and Harris and Skye were there. I noticed one of them who'd been a maid with us in Broadford in Skye was wearing my own dress! I was very taken aback. I couldn't go up and snatch it off her, and I couldn't say anything; it would be altogether too embarrassing. So I let the matter pass.

One night a crowd of us, mostly cousins, were going back to our digs or places where we lived, being dropped off one by one at the different houses. I was sharing digs with my brother Duncan and we'd arranged that we'd leave the key under the mat, because I knew I'd be late getting back. When I was dropped off and went to pick up my key from under the mat, it wasn't there! And me being a little bit tight I thought, 'Well, never mind, I'll just get in through the window.' So I went to the window, tried to pull it open or push it, push it up, but I couldn't get at the sneck, I couldn't get it open. And a policeman came along.

He said, 'What's the matter, girl?'

And I said, 'Well, I can't get in. I live here and I can't get in. I thought I'd left the key under the mat but my brother must have taken it.'

He said, 'Oh, well, never mind dear, I'll help you.' And he was a policeman, mind you! He very kindly used a great muscular arm to shove the window up, and he gave me a lift over the sill into the house, then shut the window again.

I dashed through that room into the hall and started climbing the stairs. And when I got to the first landing I noticed there was a grandfather's clock. I thought, 'Where on earth did that come from? I never saw that before.' But, never mind, I was three flights up. So I went up the next flight and there was a great big chest of drawers, brass handles. And I thought, 'Well, good lord, I've never seen that before.' And then the penny dropped. I must be in the wrong house!

Now how do I get down three flights of stairs without being heard? I thought, 'What will I do? Slide down the banister, or what?' I tried to be as quiet as a mouse but as speedy as a hare, and eventually got down to the front door, seized it open and ran out, completely out of breath. And by the grace of God nobody had heard me. So, I didn't know what to do. I thought, 'Well, it must be the next door.' The houses were so similar! And I went to the house next door, grovelled under the mat and there was the key.

There were important and interesting people you could meet in London in those days, the 1930s. For instance, one year I went to the Chelsea Arts Ball and was invited to sit on the knee of Maurice Chevalier. My escort had been introduced to him and took me up to his box, where I was invited to sit on the eminent man's knee. There were two other girls on the other knee, but it was still a very exciting occasion.

Meanwhile, I must find myself a job, but it was quite easy really, because Uncle Duncan had decided to have one-day dry cleaners all over the globe. He contacted a man called Gardner who had invented a new machine, the Burtol, for the business and thus got a shop in Wigmore Street. I was invited to come and be a student, learn the business; he thought there might be some future for me. This I did, but I was absolutely hopeless. After all, I hadn't come to London to be a shop assistant, I'd come to be a film star! So I wasn't very happy except that my cousin Aloe was in town, and my Uncle Iain used to take me to wonderful places, to wine and dine, nightclubs, and we had fun.

Life in London at this time was very exciting. I was full of drive and energy, and worked very hard in Uncle Duncan's dry cleaning shop, Spic and Span in Wigmore Street. But I was so bad at dealing with the books and any written work that I decided to go below stairs, learn about 'spotting', the various stains and all the different chemicals to use on them. But of course Uncle Duncan needed to put someone in as manageress, so he advertised; quite a number of women and men turned up to get the job.

One was Joan Denoup. She was good-looking, very sexy and also very clever, so she got the job. To be honest, she rather 'put my nose out', because, for one thing, she had fallen for Aloe; he up to now had been my companion, escorted me to all sorts of dinners, functions and nightclubs. I was going to miss him dreadfully.

The Theatrical Wren

However, I discovered through a letter from my mother that I had another cousin in London called Donald Gillies. He and his family as small children had left Plockton on the mainland, gone to America and become prosperous in fruit farming. Donald was now back in London as a director of an advertising firm, so I had a number of dates with him. He introduced me to photography and thought I would make a good model. I did well, but they paid too little; and I still wanted to get into films. So I took to going round the agents again, but wasn't very bright.

One day I saw a great long queue, hundreds of beautiful girls, waiting to get into an agent's office off Shaftesbury Avenue. I thought I'd ask them what they were after. One of the girls told me they were trying to apply for a part in a film at Elstree Studios, *The Wandering Jew*; twelve girls were needed for the tournament scene. So I queued up with the rest of them. It was a hot summer's day and I had bought off the street a toffee apple on a stick. In fact, I'd bought two of them. I was nibbling away at one, not knowing where I was going to throw the core or the stick, when I saw a window at my elbow. With hundreds of girls either side of me who didn't seem to be taking any notice, I used my elbow and pushed against the window. It wasn't locked! So I pushed it up – in the first instance I'd meant to put my apple core through, but then I thought – why don't I put myself through the window, see what happens!

So, as quick as a flash I jumped up onto the sill, jumped into the window, without realising who was inside, slammed it down again and locked it, then turned round to find that I was in the main casting office.

'What the hell . . .' said the casting director. 'Where on earth did you come from?'

And I replied, 'Skye,' which was perfectly true, of course.

71

And he just laughed and then I said, 'Would you like this toffee apple?'

And he said, 'I'd love it.' So I gave him the toffee apple. He asked me a lot of other questions – could I ride, could I swim, would I like a part in this film that they were making?

So of course I said, 'Yes, that's what I was there queuing up for, and would love it.'

He said, 'Well, you're on! Here's the address in Wardour Street to get yourself fitted up with the costume you will require. Here's another address where you go for your wig, and here's another address where you go for your shoes.'

I said, 'Well, that's all very well, but can I use your telephone? I'm broke, I haven't got my bus fare to my digs, let alone to go to all these places.'

So he laughed and gave me a pound. I was able to get a taxi, go home to my digs, and the following morning go in search of all these places; the wigmakers, the costume makers and the shoemakers. I was so excited I nearly burst. Fired with enthusiasm I promptly gave up my job at Spic and Span and started becoming a 'film extra', and forming a round robin with some other girls and boys. We took turns at going round the agents and picking up whatever we could in the way of a few lines or a small part. My contracts were for minor roles in *Hungry Hill* and *So Well Remembered*.

In one film I got quite a large part: an Irish film with Robertson Justice, and the part required Irish Gaelic. He was pretending that he could speak the language. Of course I could speak Highland Gaelic, not the Irish, but I got away with it. We had great fun on the sets. All he could say was, 'S mise bodach na fearsach' (I am the old man with the beard). He had a substantial beard, and I used to rib him a lot.

He was good company, would take me to dinner at places like Claridges, and give them a case or two of rare wine

instead of paying the bill. One day he took me to buy a
bulldozer that he was taking north! Another day we were out
together, it happened to be a Sunday, there weren't many
places open. We got on a bus to go out of town and my heel,
about six inches high, fell off my shoe. It was very embarrassing, but I was astonished to find Robertson Justice knew his
way about London, better than anyone I have ever met in my
life. I was really rather afraid of the place he took me, down an
alley, somewhere about Wardour Street, into a basement flat.
He said he knew a cobbler there, and after knocking at the
door for quite a considerable time it squeaked and creaked
and opened.

It was all sinister and very black inside, and this elderly man
with a long beard said, 'What do you want?'

Robertson Justice knew him well and said, 'This lady has
lost the heel off her shoe. Can you replace it, so we will be able
to hobble around for the rest of the day? How long will it take
you?'

So the old man said, 'Well, since it's you – I'll do it straight
away!'

We went off to a café, had a coffee and waited. I wouldn't
say we waited more than half an hour, and came back to find
that a beautiful heel matching the other one had been placed
on my shoe.

It was an advantage knowing Robertson Justice because he
was already making a name for himself. I found myself
rubbing shoulders with important people: Peter Ustinov,
Peter Laurie and Alfred Hitchcock, all sorts of odd bods of
that day and age. But there were the lean times too, as always
in the theatrical business. And so I contacted Mr Gardner of
Spic and Span and asked him if I could have a job in the dry
cleaning business somewhere other than my uncle's firm, and
he got me a job in Sloan Street.

I didn't stay there very long because there was a young man pestering and annoying me considerably. One day I took the big tin box full of needles and pins and I flung it at him. He got me bodily, flung me out in the mews. And, although I was in no way at fault really, just defending myself, I came in and said I didn't want to stay there any longer.

Meanwhile, a young man had arrived to learn the business as I had done. He wanted to learn it from 'A' to 'Z'. He was Ralph Millais, the grandson of Sir John Millais. He had opened a business in Farnham, Surrey, and invited me to come and work for him. I readily agreed as I rather liked him. He had a great sense of humour and I was very eager to get out of the Sloan Street shop. So, there down in Farnham I was introduced to Lady Millais. She was kind and invited me to their home up at Frensham Ponds more or less every weekend. Gradually, I got very fond of Sir Ralph and sent home to Skye for a couple of delightful little Skye Terrier puppies, as a present for him. But it was to be a parting present, because I'd made up my mind that if he wasn't going to pop the question soon, I'd be as well to clear out.

So I contacted Mr Gardner again and got myself a job in Guernsey in the Channel Islands, again in a dry cleaning establishment. But I was terribly lonely there, almost suicidal. In fact, I was standing at the end of the pier late at night just looking down at the water – I hadn't intended to commit suicide or anything like that, but I felt a heavy hand on my shoulder and turned to see a policeman grabbing hold of me.

'Don't do it, dear. Don't do it!' he said.

I said, 'Do what?' It was a bit embarrassing, because I don't think I was going to jump in but one never knows . . . I was depressed, so much so that I sent home to Skye asking if my cousin Ann Graham would come and join me, and her brother Iain. They readily agreed, travelled south and came over to

Guernsey. I asked my boss to fit them in to his shop. We had fun together doing all sorts of mad things but I was offered a job with more money and more prospects in Jersey, so I left Guernsey.

But I was more lonely now than ever. So I wrote to my mother, she came down and joined me in Jersey. We took trips over to St Malo and Dinard in France and it was a very pleasant time. I also had a boyfriend, but I didn't like him much and nobody else did either; he wore kid gloves that seemed to me a little sinister in a young man. I wondered if he intended to throttle me one dark night. However, round about this time Aloe had become engaged to Joan Denoup and I was invited to the wedding, naturally! I sailed back to London – we were all there, mother, too – and it was a very beautiful occasion. I drank an enormous amount of champagne, and the tears flowed more easily.

I didn't return to the Channel Islands. Instead I took a job as a florist in Old Bond Street. That was exciting. The Woolworth's heiress Barbara Hutton was having a baby, and I was detailed to arrange the flowers in a hotel for a banquet. I remember making up all kinds of wreaths, corsages and décor. Barbara Hutton was a fussy lady, demanding that I compose something with daisies, buttercups and country flowers, very difficult to find at the time. We sent everywhere – even to the Channel Islands – and did what we could to find the flowers.

My cousins Iain and Ann decided to come back from the Channel Islands, and while mother was still in town we managed to buy a house in Earls Court to be shared together. My mother's sister Chrissie came through from Skye. Mother and she must have given us the wherewithal to maintain this large flat. So there we were. Two more cousins joined us from Skye, Ena Graham and my sister June and we were a houseful!

We had a whale of a time just painting London red, so young and bright and ridiculous when you think of it.

The weather seemed to be always good, we girls used to go up to the top of the roof, sunbathe in the costumes we wore then – bikinis had not become fashionable. We'd lie out on rugs on the roof, then later all go to the cinema. One evening while up there we whispered to each other, 'Let's go to the cinema and leave Ena behind.' I don't know what Ena had done to be put in the doghouse, but we crept down and left her snoring away.

Off we went to the cinema, but she woke up and noticed, saw us leaving the house and was furious. She ran downstairs, grabbed the first thing she could find, a fur coat, flung it on and ran after us. So we all got into a pew in the cinema, the lights went off and the film began. Suddenly Ena became very agitated: we realised that her nose was bleeding like mad and it wouldn't stop. We all gave her our handkerchiefs but that wasn't enough. She just bled and bled, so we summoned the usherette and she carted Ena off to the manager's office. Ann and myself followed, into the office where she was stretched out on a table clutching her fur coat to her. We couldn't really understand this; she needed to get some air and we needed to put towels round her, and so on. So somebody flung her coat open – to our horror there she was in a very brief bathing costume! Now of course it is hilariously funny, but at the time it was utterly shame-making.

Around this time I became friends with a lady called Madame Crichton, whom I had met a few years back in Skye. She had stayed at Liveras with us, and was particularly impressed with me having a row with the minister's son, had overheard our conversation and been rather intrigued with the way I went about giving that lad a piece of my mind. When I went back into the house she'd said, 'Any time you're in London come and see me, because I would like to give you a course of theatre training.'

This seemed a good time to look the old opera singer up. She took me along to meet Madame Touraine of the Webber Douglas School of Dramatic Art. It all took place in the Chanticlear Theatre and of course I was thrilled to death. That doesn't mean to say I improved in any way, with the advantage of these lessons. Madame Crichton paid for them and I did my best but I wasn't really very good at anything. When I was taught a stage trick – you put one foot in front of the other and pretend to trip – I couldn't even do that properly. So I gave it up!

I appeared as an extra in several more films; the clerk (at a special rate of five pounds per day) in *Odd Man Out*, *The 39 Steps* and others. Of course I took any kind of job I could get betwixt and between. I went one day to a big furnishing company; walking in the door I saw a long ladder up to a high ceiling. At the very top was a tiny little lady painting, and I was fascinated. I stood and watched her as she made cupids, angels, wild horses and Greek designs – painting away madly.

Then I was going to move into the place when she shouted out to me, 'Stop! Don't move an inch, can't you see – I'm painting you!'

And I said, 'Oh good lord, I didn't realise that you were.'

'Yes,' she said, 'I want your face in this!' And then down her great long ladder she came and said, 'Would you allow me to continue painting? Could you come tomorrow and just stand where you are, let me put you into this mural? My name is Beatrice MacDairmid.'

Well, of course it was a job and I presumed she would pay me, so I said, 'Well, yes, I'd like that very much.'

She gave me her address and told me to come to her studio. The following day I went, I was very impressed with her. She

was a charming little lady, we had brioche and coffee, everything was smart and Bohemian; it was a new world for me. She
asked if she might paint my portrait; so there I was again,
sitting, for another three portraits. God knows where they are
now, I never claimed them.

On one of the days when I was sitting her husband came in,
and as far as I could see there was no love lost between them.
But he asked me about myself, what I did. I told him I had
done a bit of acting, understudied at the Embassy Theatre,
this and that. And he said, 'Well, would you like to come and
understudy down at the Arts Theatre, Cambridge?'

'Yes, please, that would be wonderful.'

So off I went to Cambridge, meeting so many professionals,
and it was most intriguing. We did a series of Noel Coward
plays. I must have been awfully bad in the small parts they
gave me, and I wasn't very comfortable there because some of
the actors and actresses were very snooty. I felt self-conscious
and uncomfortable most of the time.

Round about the same time I met up again with Gerald
Peel, a boy who used to come to Skye every summer. He was
at Cambridge and invited me to May Week. We sailed along
the Cam, well, when I say 'sail' I think we rowed. And we ate
chickens, drank champagne, had strawberries and cream
galore; I ate cherries until I was sick, and then we danced
in the evening – eightsome reels all over Cambridge in the
middle of the road and in the square – we had a wonderful
time! The police came after us and we grabbed a hold of them,
made them take part in the eightsomes, really quite fun!

Meanwhile, changes were taking place rapidly up north. My
grandmother had died, and my mother, feeling that she never
saw her family – her large flock of five children – decided to
buy a house in Glasgow in Kersland Street. This was 1939,
and I came up to help mother decorate and furnish the place.

Also I presented myself to the BBC in Glasgow, hoping that they would take me for their BBC rep, to do some broadcasting in the drama section. I was lucky enough to meet Moultrie Kelsall. He was very generous with work and I had quite a number of parts, mostly in the Highland plays.

Back home in Skye Liveras was now empty; Auntie Belle, Uncle Duncan's wife, sold it to one of the Robertson family for peanuts. This was shattering for me because I had loved Liveras and hated to think that it was no longer ours. So whenever we went north again we went to stay in Grandma's new house in Breakish, which I didn't like nearly so much as the original.

Meanwhile back in Glasgow the Great Exhibition was underway and my sister Morag and myself took a job running a beauty salon. There was a feverish feeling in the air and nobody ever seemed to know what was going to happen from one day to the next. It was no longer easy to get on to Skye, it had become a restricted area; you could neither get off it nor to it without a special permit. And War was declared. So the family, all of us, joined up. I decided to be on the mending end, volunteering as a Red Cross nurse in Lennox Castle.

People were being evacuated from Glasgow in their hundreds. They started with babies. I had to nurse hundreds of babies, all of them with enteritis. I caught the enteritis myself and was pretty ill. But I had to keep going because the Clydebank Blitz came down on us. Uncle Duncan had presented ambulances to Glasgow and the casualties were brought out to Lennox Castle in their hundreds. There were five operating tables going at the one time.

I was asked to assist with one poor devil who had been buried for days and days under the rubble and had lost part of his leg. They had to re-amputate it further up and then further up again, and I had to stand by – I can't remember what I was asked to do. Whatever it was I didn't see much of it, because I fell into a dead faint and had to be carried out of the operating theatre by the Boy Scouts who were mentally defective – the major part of the Castle itself was a mental home. But some of the patients were good enough, able to be stretcher-bearers, and they were also Boy Scouts. So they put me on a stretcher, carried me out of the operating theatre and, would you believe it, placed me on top of a high wall. And me unconscious! When I came to I was aghast to find myself perched away up high without a clue in the world how to get down.

The nursing was very exhausting indeed. Old women were brought out from Glasgow from old people's homes and poor houses, and they seemed to be as ancient as God to me. They thought nothing of relieving themselves (both kinds) in their beds, and would wander about, obstreperous, really very difficult to cope with.

As everyone was terribly busy and there was far too much to do, the nursing sisters were allowed to give these patients shots of stuff called paraldehyde to calm them down. Every night the nursing sisters would be going round giving injections of this stuff to all these old biddies to keep them from climbing the walls: every time the sirens went off they would get over-excited.

None of the nurses had enough time to go through to Glasgow or anywhere else to get their hair done, for instance. So I decided it would be a good idea to ask the matron if I could have part of one of the wards cornered off with screens, volunteering to hand paint them myself in Beatrice MacDairmid style, with cupids, angels and horses. I used the lockers from the wards as dressing tables, put mirrors above them, found out which and how many of the nurses had had any experience in hairdressing. There were one or two who had been expert hairdressers before joining up, so I got them together and we ran this beauty salon, for three hundred nurses in fact. It was quite an experience, but very exhausting; that, together with the nursing I had to do all day and, very often, all night.

So I began to see things, get night nurse's paralysis, imagine there was a mouse's tail in my pudding and things like that. I got extremely ill, and was sent back to Skye to recuperate. I was very soon fit as a fiddle again; that's what Skye does to you. It's so bracing and such a wonderful island you can't be ill for long.

Instead of going back to the nursing I decided to join the Wrens (Women's Royal Naval Service) in Glasgow. My sister was now a Wren officer at St Enoch's Hotel and I decided to see if she could put in a word for me. And she did so. Then I was sent to Mill Hill in London for training, to find out which part of the service I would be put in. They asked me many questions. When they realised I came from Skye they said, 'I think you would be good on boats.' And I said, 'That would be spiffing,' and they sent me to Richmond, Surrey. I was detailed off, to get my training on the Thames under the supervision of the famous author, politician and director A P Herbert, on his notorious boat *The Water Gypsy* about which he had written a book (see plate 13).

But there were no shenanigans on his boat in those days. It was serious training, with five of a crew, all girls. He was good to us, very amusing, and he used to take us into the House of Commons, all round, tell us about everything. Together with our training from A P Herbert a few of us were put on the bridges on the Thames. They put me on Westminster Bridge. We had a little hut in the middle where we were supposed to observe everything and report back to Richmond what we saw, what would fall and where.

Before going to our post on the middle of the bridge we were put into various institutes and buildings. I was often put into the Hovis factory and sometimes it would be the Tate & Lyle factory. There we would be given a sort of trestle bed. Not a bed really; it was a piece of canvas on a metal frame where we would lie down until the sirens went off. When they went off, we were dressed of course; we had to take our whistle, all our equipment, our gas masks and run like mad to the very middle of our bridge – observe everything that was happening.

Some of the places they put us in for this waiting game were horrific. I think one was an ICI building, in the cellars, and there was no air. I don't know what was wrong with the equipment that gives artificial air, but nothing was coming through; I remember I nearly died one night with no oxygen. Another night they put me in a place, I don't know what it was, they had animals for testing: weasels and rats and things all in a row in cages, in a building on the Thames. I took one look at it and said to someone, 'I cannot sleep or rest in here. There is no way.' I ran out of the place and had my cape with me. I lay on one of the benches on the Thames, covered myself completely, head and all, so that nobody would know and anyone passing would think I was just a drunk. I got away with that until the morning. But it was horrific.

There was the brighter side of it, of course: the girls from the other bridges and myself would go to the Seven Bells, a well-known pub on the Thames and have a few drinks. We did that a few times, but unfortunately some old cow reported us and we weren't allowed to go there again.

I was then transferred down to Plymouth, to be with a crew of four other girls on a little cutter that ran between the big ships. We girls took depth charges and the like out to the ships moored in Plymouth, such as the FS *Paris* and many

American warships. The FS *Paris* was a beautiful old ship and I was fascinated by the ornate gimbals and furnishings of her salon. But from time to time I had to take punishment, because the captain of HMS *Pembroke*, the mother ship, disapproved when Moultrie Kelsall would send for me from Glasgow to go and do broadcasts on programmes entitled 'Women on the Guns'. When I went to ask permission to travel north I would sometimes be refused. That used to make me very angry. If an ordinary able-bodied sailor asked for permission to be let off to play football, it was immediately granted. So I thought it was jolly unfair, and I didn't hesitate to say so.

On one occasion I was sent ashore for punishment to Wren Quarters, next door to a Norwegian barracks. I was told that I had to stitch bedspreads, peel potatoes and do gardening. So one day when I was told to do the gardening as a punishment – it was rotten weather and I couldn't get the leaves burnt off – I got a tin of paraffin from the shed, poured this all along the hedge that divided our house from the barracks and set the whole thing on fire. Well, it was a wonderful horo-gheallaidh because all the men came bounding out to beat the flames and all the girls came bounding out from our side to beat the boys, so to speak! So we had a rare old time of it and I was severely punished after that, I can assure you.

One night near Christmas time some of our crew, including myself, were invited on board a submarine for dinner. It was a very nice affair and the men were gentlemen who in no way abused the situation; but, nevertheless, we did have quite a number of drinks. And I can't drink too much without getting a bit heady. So we overstepped the time, I had to be back on shore by midnight and I hadn't managed to do that. So how on earth was I going to get back into the building? I decided to try the downstairs lavatory window, managed to open it and scrambled up – I was good at that – got in through the window and fell bang into the arms of the leading Wren officer.

'Right, Wren Sykes,' she said, 'where have you been?'

And I staggered out, saluted her and said, 'Midnight mass-sh, ma'am.' I got more punishment the next day.

Every morning on a shore base there would be prayers called Divisions. And rightly so, because the officer taking the service would shout out, 'All C of Es line up; other denominations fall out,' and of course all the Roman Catholics were dismissed. When they were dismissed they went down to the village, to Richmond, to the nearest café and consumed an enormous amount of soggy cream cakes, delicious!

I had a sneaking interest in Roman Catholicism although I would never dare say so in Skye. Most Sgitheanaichs are anti-Catholic or were in my day. My fondness for cream cakes was not my only reason for siding with the Roman Catholics in the Wrens. Memories of my days long before in Hoylake and in the Liverpool Arts School, where I had been sent briefly, before we settled in Skye made a big impact on my imagination.

I used to travel from Five-Lamps House, where we lived between Crosby and Waterloo, into Liverpool on an electric train to the Liverpool Arts School. I remember I was very nervous, having never been to a proper school in my life; surrounded by such a quantity of students was very intimidating. On my first day we all went for a break to a sort of large kitchen in the Arts School, to have a snack or bite of lunch. We all had to scramble for it and a domestic was there who helped to scramble eggs or poach them, make up sandwiches, and I decided on a poached egg, unfortunately. This girl handed it to me and there was a big, tall, blonde beauty of a girl who was scrambling for a sandwich or something and she quite deliberately bumped into me, knocked my hand and the poached egg fell onto the floor. I was mortified; my first day, what a terrible thing to happen.

But a little girl, very dark and rather pretty, came bounding over to help me and I realised that she was a Spaniard. Her name was Manuella. She whispered to me that the blonde was a right bitch and, of course, I fully agreed with her. So from that time onwards Manuella and myself were very good friends, and we did all we could to avoid being bullied by the tall blonde. Manuella took me home to her parents' house and I stayed weekends there from time to time. Next door to her was a girl called Chi-Chi, with eleven brothers, so, of course the contact was very interesting. They used to have wonderful parties down in a cellar where they dished up coffee from a big fish kettle. My friendship with Manuella found a connection with my new Catholic friends in the Wrens.

Meanwhile, my sister Morag, back in Scotland, was working on secret documents in the St Enoch's Hotel, and there she met a naval officer called Nigel Johnston who invited her to dinner on board his ship together with the girl she was working with. Morag fell in love with Nigel and vice versa; later on Morag was sent to Oban, and Nigel's ship came into Oban where they fell even more in love, and got engaged to be married.

Now he at the time was a Roman Catholic, but as he was captain of his ship he had to take Divisions on board and hated the idea of making the RCs fall out. So he decided not to be an RC any more and adopted the Protestant religion. It was a bit of a mix-up because his mother was still alive in New Zealand,

and she had sent a message to tell Nigel that he must be married as a Catholic! Morag, of course, was not a Catholic. They got permission to be married in Brompton Oratory in London, and I was to be the one and only bridesmaid.

It was very interesting but very confusing in those days; the Catholics were very strict about non-Catholics and I was only allowed to go up to, I think, the fourth altar. I wasn't allowed to continue up to the top altar with my sister when she was married. So there I was, stuck, in the flowers way down the aisle while Morag and Nigel proceeded forward to be married. There was a wonderful reception afterwards at the Hyde Park Hotel. My poor father had an enormous bill because there were a lot of gatecrashers, particularly those uninvited people from various ships on the Thames at the time.

But the cake was a great success! I had presented that, got it made through my very good contact with the Hovis and the Tate & Lyle companies in whose premises I had been sheltering during the days guarding the bridges of London. It was a very ornate work of art with four tiers, an icing ship on top and lots of little sailors in sugar icing. It lasted a long while, as Morag would yank it out every time a new child was born; she was to have four children, and the cake would come in useful for many years to come.

My cousin Donald Gillies from America was my escort at the wedding and during my stay in London at that time. I learnt with great unhappiness that he had developed cancer; very soon after that he died. I was devastated. After the wedding I returned to Plymouth for the remainder of the War, or almost the remainder . . . and I will tell now how I disgraced myself. I tell it sometimes with pride and sometimes with shame, and this is how it happened.

I had applied for a transfer to Rosyth because, after all, my people were in Scotland. The request was denied me. Everything seemed to be denied me these days and I was very upset and distressed. On my last leave, for instance, I stayed in Glasgow, and Moultrie Kelsall at the BBC had asked me to go and visit Neil Gunn, the author, because Moultrie thought I would be very suitable to play the part of Catherine in *The Silver Darlings*, a film they were going to make. If Neil Gunn approved he was quite sure that I would get the job.

So I made my way up north and met this charming man, indeed he was awfully nice to me. We went for a long walk together, discussed the character of the leading part in the film, and Neil Gunn thought I would be ideally suitable. I felt, oh, so buoyant, so happy. We went along to the railway line and leaned over the fence. Neil Gunn told me that whenever he was a bit depressed, whenever he was trying to think out a new story or planning anything, he always came to that spot, just beside the railway; he would lean on the fence and look along the line as far as he could see, reaching far, far up to the North. I just had a lot in common with the man. I felt so proud to have met him and went back to London in great haste to see the director.

The wretched director said, 'Oh no, I've made other plans. I'm sorry, I'm quite sure that you would be right for the part in every other way but there's one way in which you are not right, that is, you haven't a sufficiently big name. I have already spoken to Patricia Rock and offered her the part.'

I could have killed him there and then. However, I just had to bear it and get back to Plymouth to my ship, the HMS *Pembroke*. Once again I agitated and asked to be transferred to Rosyth. The captain said this time, 'Oh, you will be transferred in the morning. You'd better get packed!' And, my God, I got packed and when I was given the chits I would require, all the paperwork, didn't it say I was to be transferred to HMS *Albatross*, a ship across the plank from us! I was absolutely furious, but could do nothing about it, so I transferred to HMS *Albatross*.

I think the petty officer there must have been told to take the mickey out of me: he put me on a job I'd never had to do before, scrub down half a dozen small craft all in a row. I had to start with the first and scrub one after another, till I'd finished the job. Well, I started on number one – it was a very hot day. Then number two, then number three, and, oh my God! I was sweating, pushing my titfer, the bonnet we wore, to the back of my head. And this petty officer shouted to me, 'Wren Sykes, put your titfer on straight!' So I did, and then it slid back again as I was scrubbing, scrubbing away, the sweat pouring off my brow. He shouted to me again, 'Wren Sykes, put your titfer on straight!'

I did so, then it slid back again. And again he shouted at me. But this time I found myself standing up stiff, like a poker, and my arm wouldn't move for me to salute, my body was completely numb. I did not put my titfer on straight. Instead of that I climbed off the boat and started walking towards the petty officer, quite close to him, right past him, under his nose, and started to walk away towards the cast iron gates in the far distance. And I kept on walking, walking and he yelled at me, 'Come back! I'll only ask you three times and then you'll be shot.'

I took no notice – I couldn't take any notice, I just couldn't do anything rather than what I was doing, to walk, walk, and walk away. He yelled again, 'On the third request you will be shot, if you don't obey.'

And I found some little voice in the back of my head saying, 'Shoot, you bugger, shoot! I couldn't care less.' I kept on walking until I reached the great gates and walked through them, on and on until I reached the railway station. I didn't even go back to the quarters on shore for my gear. I went straight up to the railway station. I seemed to come to there when a saucy, fat, old girl from the WVS (Women's Voluntary Service) handed me a jam jar of hot tea, because in those days all kinds of jars were used to give the troops a free cup of tea on the stations and a sandwich, or a biscuit.

I was grateful for that, drank it down and then got on the train – I don't think I had a ticket even, I just got on. There was a sailor in the carriage. He seemed a nice lad there in the far corner, and I just sat, still very numb. He started to talk so I started to talk too, and I told him what had happened. He said, 'You're jolly right. You did the right thing. I would have done the same myself.'

Then it hit me – I was a deserter! My God, what was going to happen to me? And the guilty feeling started. The train was underway and there was nothing I could do except arrive in London. So I sat on a bench, thought and thought, 'Could I continue on to Skye?' No. I had no pass. What on earth could I do? So, gradually, I decided to give myself up. Well, who to? I hadn't a clue who you gave yourself up to when you were a deserter.

Then I thought about the Port of London Authority, a great big building that I'd recognised on the Thames: 'Well, I'll go there and ask for the chief of Wrens, Mrs Lawton Matthews.' What a cheek I had! Anyway, this I did. I had a little money so I got in a taxi, told the driver to take me to the Port of London Authority buildings. I got there, had a bit of difficulty being shown in to the chief of Wrens, if she was the chief of Wrens, and I very much doubt it. But that's what they said she was. I went in, started to confess that I had deserted from Plymouth and I now felt very guilty, very ashamed; I would take whatever punishment they wanted to mete out; I was prepared to go back and apologise, get on with my job.

She was awfully nice and said, 'Well, you obviously can't be very well.'

And I said, 'Yes, I'm perfectly well, I'm quite fit. I'm awfully tired though.'

'Yes, dear, you must be awfully tired. Now of course we'll take you back, and of course we understand the situation perfectly. But there is one thing, it is a regulation that if anything like this happens, the person has to see a psychiatrist before going back.'

I said, 'What? A psychiatrist? But there's nothing wrong with my mind.'

'I know, dear,' she said, 'I know. You're probably perfectly sane, but it is a regulation, and we have to keep to the regulations. So I'm afraid you can't be taken back until you have seen a psychiatrist.'

I said, 'Thank you ma'am', saluted, turned on my heel and walked out. Found my way back to Euston Station and sat on a bench there for a very long time, when who should come up but that lad who had been in my carriage when I came up from Plymouth!

He sat down beside me and said, 'Well, how are you getting on?'

And I said, 'Well, I'm not. I have really deserted this time.' I told him that I had been to see the Wren Officer, she'd said I'd have to see a psychiatrist, and all that rubbish. So now I didn't have enough money to get back to Scotland as a civilian, and I had no pass. I didn't know what to do.

And he said, 'Well, look, I've got a pass that would take me as far as Inverness, but I've no intention of going because I've fallen in love with a girl here in London, and I want to spend my leave with her. So you're very welcome to my pass if you think you can get away with it.'

'Well,' I said, 'I think it's worth a try.' And believe it or not

this is what I did! I simply kept my thumb over the name of
the sailor and, with one pass looking much the same as
another, I got away with it.

And found myself, of all people, stopped at the station
barrier by Lord MacDonald of the Isles, whom I knew quite
well! He'd been a frequent visitor at Skeabost and was very
friendly with my father. So I chatted to him, asked him all
about Skye and what was going on, kept blethering away until
it was time for the train to leave. I then said to him, 'Oh gosh I
must go. Gosh, I'll only just catch the train.' So I didn't show
my pass at all and jumped on the northbound train.

To my horror it stopped at Dingwall, and everybody had to
get out because the portion I was in was going only to the
Black Isle. There I was, stuck again, sans ticket, sans anything,
certainly not enough money to go to a hotel and it was the
weekend; there were no trains going to Kyle of Lochalsh. So I
told a tale of woe to the station master who was a nice old
body. He took his lamp – it was getting late now – and he said,
'Well, it so happens there's a troop train going through with
Polish soldiers, and I'll stop it for you.'

So he got onto the line, waved his lantern backwards and
forwards, stopped the train, legged me up on board. To my
astonishment I found myself amongst more than a hundred
Polish soldiers, none of whom, as far as I could make out, could
speak a word of English! And I certainly couldn't speak a word
of Polish. But there I was, and one of them very politely bowed,
clicked his heels and gave me his seat. And that's how I got to
Kyle of Lochalsh, and then of course the ferry – I never paid on
it anyway – and got across to Skye (see plate 21).

My mother and father were living in the new house Cnoc
Gorm at the time in Breakish. I told them that I badly needed
to hide from the authorities, from the Wrens. They gave me
enough money and I decided to go and stay with Annie

Finlayson in Bru Barvas in Stornoway, the one who'd been my mother's help in Hoylake for so many years.

That's what I did. I enjoyed that stay in Bru Barvas immensely. It sticks in my mind to this day, walking through the machair and along the coast where the great big breakers crashed onto the black rocks on this very rugged coastline. I always remember the white doves dashing out from the cavities in the rocks and soaring up in the wind. It was quite magical and Annie Finlayson's mother was alive in those days. She was a very tiny woman, I suppose she would be a dwarf, was always lifted onto a high stool. She took me into the sitting room – the room that's never used except for funerals and weddings and that sort of thing, most of the people there at that time lived in the kitchen – and said in Gaelic that she had a big surprise for me. A treat. And she opened a big cupboard, pulled out a box, and out of the box was brought an orange! We sat by the peat fire, specially lit on account of my staying there, and we ate the orange between us, a huge treat. I don't think they'd ever had oranges before.

At that time (1944) the Hebrides was pronounced a restricted area, and I wondered how I would get back to town again. I felt now the heat would be off, the recruiting officers would no longer be looking for me. Finally, at the end of the War, I did get an Honourable Discharge from the Wrens. But, for the present, I wanted to get back to my theatrical career. So my mother sent for me, said there had been a telegram from the BBC in Glasgow asking me to take part in a play called *The Shetland Bus*. A very interesting play, the author was there; it was an all male cast. And I was lucky to have that telegram because the BBC could do miracles: I didn't need a pass to go south and take part in that play.

While I was in Glasgow I took on quite a few parts, joined the Scottish National Players and met people like Jean Taylor

Smith and Mollie Urquhart, Fulton MacKay and all the gang. I seemed to get on quite well with them, got several bits and pieces of parts. Then James Bridie met me one day in the Automobile Club and offered me the job of wardrobe mistress and assistant stage manager at the Citizens Theatre in Alhambra. Of course I jumped at the chance. This was the beginning, I thought, of a career I had been all my life hoping to enter.

In those days I played many parts in real life too. I became a beauty specialist for a firm called Beauty Bars Ltd at the Empire Exhibition in Bellahouston. I also took a job in a photographer's in Byres Road. Mother and father came through to Glasgow as mother wanted to sell the house in Kersland Street and take on a long lease of a flat in Havelock Street. And having moved with the company under the direction of Eric Capon we moved from the Alhambra into the Citizens Theatre proper, as it is today. I enjoyed my work there under the caring eye of Elspeth Cochrane. I got lots of small parts in a number of plays – *The Government Inspector* and Ibsen's play *Hedda Gabler* – and I tried to be as helpful as I could. In fact, I helped the designer with all the costumes (see plate 8).

Later on, mother again got itchy feet, and decided to share a great house, Langarth in Stirling, with my sister Morag and her husband Nigel. Nigel had been promoted and was made liaison officer for New Zealand, working for Lord Mountbatten. Langarth was a beautiful house, large enough for us to do a lot of things. I enjoyed and monopolised the attics, had a four-poster bed and a very ornate music stand, and started to learn to play the violin under the tuition of Professor Arkley. He had a glass eye, was a good deal older than myself, and used to go over to France and bring back perfume.

One summer we actresses went on tour with the Citizens Theatre, the play *Hedda Gabler*. John Duncan MacRae was in it, Dennis Carey and his wife Yvonne Collette. We had a wonderful time and were successful. I only had a tiny bit in it, the maid, but was thrilled with the experience. When we came back I did a spell with the Perth Repertory Company, played the part of Mrs Joe Gargerry in Charles Dickens' play *Great Expectations*. A fantastic experience, I did enjoy!

Then the Citizens Theatre was offered the chance to join ENSA and go abroad to entertain the troops. They were considered to be a number one company, so we had to travel to London, go to Drury Lane, where we were kitted out with, believe it or not, army officers' uniforms. I became a lieutenant with two pips up, very pleased with myself! There was one shattering occasion when my little sister June, who was in the Army in Edinburgh, was being transferred to Wales; she came through London to see me and we met at the corner of Drury Lane. She was a sergeant. There I was standing up straight as a ramrod in my new uniform; she came up to me, said, 'If you think I'm bloody well going to salute you, you've got another think coming, mate!'

We went off to have lunch in a peculiar café that was halfway under the ground – I can't remember what it was called but theatrical people went there a lot; there were photographs all round the walls of famous people. It was about the time when we had to parade for Edward VIII and the death of his father.

So, there we were embarking on a ship to take us to Ostend; go by train thereafter to Paris, where we were booked in for the Théatre Comédie Française. I was understudying the girl who was to be the juvenile lead. And holy smoke, when we got aboard the ship didn't she start to be terribly ill! She was put in the captain's cabin, we were underway and Dennis Carey was in charge. We asked, 'For heaven's sake, can we have the doctor?' And they said there was no doctor on board.

So they shoved me into the cabin with the girl and, really, my job was to keep her alive some way or another. She had acute asthma and simply couldn't breathe. I did everything I could, loosened her clothes, breathed in her mouth, it was really traumatic and worrying. When we got to Ostend they put her on a stretcher and into an ambulance, and Dennis Carey shoved me in with her. There I was alone with the patient and I yelled at Dennis, 'For God's sake come with me! I have no French, I don't speak French!'

And he said, 'Neither do I.'

Off I went and we got her into hospital somehow, then of course I had to leave her there. They couldn't tell me how long she would be ill, and I had to find my way back, to the hotel we were booked into at Ostend. That night there was a knock on my bedroom door and in came Dennis with a half bottle of Scotch. He said, 'Now for God's sake, Rhona, drink this, and be word perfect in the morning as we rehearse on the train.' And he left me.

I was a very slow learner and it was a complete nightmare, I didn't know a word of the part of the play. We were very surprised when we got to Paris to be put in the same hotel as Dame Sybil Thorndyke, Ralph Richardson, Sir Laurence Olivier and others. No wonder we'd been given officers' uniforms! So we had to watch our Ps and Qs.

But they were friendly and towards the end of our stay we got very matey, indeed we all ended up dancing eightsome reels in the middle of the street. Everyone seemed to be mildly pro-Scottish. Sir Ralph Richardson was playing the leading part in Richard III, also at the Comédie Française. We, of course, moved on to other places, Dinarde and to the south of France, then got the train to Brussels; then to places in Germany, Hamburg, Lübeck and Flensburg, all intriguing and fascinating.

We saw a good deal of France. On one occasion we were invited to the castle of a distinguished baroness. I never felt so embarrassed in my life, not understanding the language; everybody was speaking French at the luncheon party. I simply couldn't join in. So I promised myself when I got back to Britain, if I ever did, the first thing I would do would be to learn French. When I was young I shared a French governess with my cousins Catriona and Jack in Skeabost, but I had never bothered to take in the tuition, except, of course, the everyday words.

We were a very happy-go-lucky bunch! Molly Urquhart in particular kept us in a lot of laughter, so did John Duncan MacRae. One day Molly was down on the sands in Lübeck. She lost her wedding ring, made a tremendous to-do about it and said she would never be able to face her husband when she got back home: it must be found, whatever happened, it simply must be!

So somehow the army got to hear about it, the British army of course. They took the machines they had for finding metal under the ground, skirted all the edge of the seashore, searched and searched, till in fact they did find her ring. She was so relieved it isn't true! All the time we were in Germany Molly seemed to be very excited and nervous. She was afraid the Germans were going to kill us, kept on believing there were lumps of glass in her pudding, would never eat it, for fear of being cut to bits.

When we got to Germany, at first we were deeply resented by a regiment of Welsh Guards who were frightfully snooty. One day we were having lunch, they rose up from their table, came across and were very insulting to Jameson Clark, Dennis Carey, Tom Maguire and other men that were with us. They started to fight and they fought like mad. We women had to hide under the tables while the men just fought until they made mincemeat of each other. But I am glad to say our company won, hands down!

Funnily enough they then showed us a lot of respect and came to each of our performances in the theatre. I ploughed my way through the leading part as best I could. It wasn't too difficult in character, a Highland girl, a Bridie play called *The Forrigan Reel*. But one disastrous thing had happened when we first set foot on German soil: we found that our skips with all our costumes had been stolen, quite literally. But the theatre we were playing in had been used by the Nazis for making uniforms; in the attics were still about twelve sewing machines and bales and bales of German uniform material. So, as I was in charge of the skips, I decided the only thing we could do was to hire some of these German professional tailors, or whatever they were, get them to make up kilts, kilt jackets and all the costumes for the whole cast -- out of this German material – which they did. But, of course, they knew nothing about tartan or anything like that, so together with one of the German hands I decided that the best thing to do was to put the costumes on the players, then paint the tartans with raw paint. So we did that. And we painted the buttons, the sporrans, everything, just painted on. You would never believe it, but it was tremendously effective (see plate 7).

Some of us were rather reluctant to leave Germany but our time was up. We had made quite a few friends amongst our enemies. I had even got a proposal of marriage from a tall, blond, handsome German naval officer. Our lot had been invited on board a big ship we had acquired, for our country, presumably. I was quite reluctant about turning him down, but he did give me a couple of souvenirs, a swastika and a little dagger with a German eagle. When I got back to Britain I'm afraid I flogged them, and got a good price too.

We were excited to find that we were to be taken back to

Britain in a Stirling bomber; quite a number of us and practically no seating – just a narrow ledge round the belly of the plane. So, as I had never in my life cared much to be squashed in amongst other people, I tried to find a seat for myself on my very shiny leather suitcase, facing the nose of the plane. After we'd taken off, suddenly there was a jolt, I slid off my leather suitcase right down into the nose of the plane, completely spreadeagled.

It was some sort of plastic because I could see through it, all round, down and down into the depths of the ocean. All the way across Holland all the way across the Channel – I was almost like a seagull – seeing everything, penetrating down into the depths of the ocean. It was terrifying! I was absolutely numb with fear and had to remain like that until we got back to Britain. It just shows you how little charisma I must have possessed as nobody even noticed that I'd disappeared. Or, if they did, they didn't think about looking for me.

We played the ancient theatre in Bath before going up to London, an uncanny experience. I was in charge of all the costumes and, in this amazing theatre, which we were very honoured to be allowed to perform in, I found the wardrobe premises were tucked away up in the roof. You had to clamber over all sorts of ropes, props, sets and equipment into a spooky little room where there was an ironing board and things for maintaining the wardrobe in an impeccable con-dition.

I remember being in there entirely alone very late one evening, hearing noises like women weeping, men laughing and glasses clinking. Of course there was nobody, so it was all very weird. I did learn afterwards, the place was haunted. I learnt this living in theatrical digs, and it was an eye-opener. I was very timid at first because one had to eat and mix with all sorts of professional theatrical people. The landlady was

proud of her guests, had photographs all over the walls of
eminent actors like George Formby and Dame Flora Robson.
Everybody that mattered in the theatrical world had apparently stayed there. Whether it was true or not I really never
knew.

The whole company found themselves booked in at Sad-
dlers Wells, very exciting. The cast had been changed
around a lot – Alastair Sim was to play the leading part.
Of course, all the costumes that had been made in Germany,
specially with German cloth and painted by myself and some
of the others, had to be thrown aside. New costumes were
booked for the play *The Forrigan Reel*, which required the
Highland kilt, jackets, sporrans, sgian dubh and all the rest of
it. They were madly immaculate and quite wrong. It would
have been far better to have stuck to the hand-painted jobs,
because the play itself was unreal, with folklore and imaginary material Bridie had written. All this hired stuff was
completely wrong.

So, with the change of cast, one thing and another, we
found we were not appreciated; the play had to come off after
about two weeks, which was very sad. Then we all split up.
Everybody while they were in London had engaged themselves to other companies, and I was at a bit of a loss. I was all
right, I knew where I could stay; my brother Chris had
become engaged to a very pretty girl, Ann MacSween, who
invited me to stay with her. So I was able to pick up broadcasts. I had a tiny part in the radio drama *The Forsyth Saga*,
other bits and pieces and understudied at the Embassy Theatre.

Around about that time (1946) VE Day was celebrated in
great style. I'd been invited to dinner to the Hungarian
Restaurant with a boyfriend, and the violinist was playing
at my table, very romantic with candles, when VE Day was

declared! The violinists and everyone rose up in the restaurant, barged through the doors into the streets. There was a wild and hilarious party, universal, everybody joining in, strangers and all kinds of people. I clung to my partner in case I should be trodden upon, it was very exciting. Indeed there were many exciting days in London at that time. But I got homesick, wanted to go back to Scotland and rejoin the Citizens Theatre. I missed the smell of the greasepaint.

Home at this time was Langarth, Stirling. Morag and Nigel who were sharing this colossal house were packing and preparing to go to New Zealand and the house was obviously going to be too big for mother and father. So mother and father were negotiating to buy a smaller house in Rothesay, Bute. Meanwhile, I was doing quite a number of broadcasts for Moultrie Kelsall and had rejoined the Citizens Theatre, where I was given the lead in a Bridie play, the part of a Russian princess (see plate 10).

I was thrilled to bits of course, but very nervous, and the travelling backwards and forwards every day and every night between Stirling and Glasgow was tedious. One of the actors had developed mumps. I caught it from him and had to be isolated in the attics of Langarth with sheets at the bottom of the stairs to prevent anybody coming through to get anywhere near me. And there were bats coming down the chimney! I was very ill and frightened, and didn't go back to the Citizens for a long time after that.

Although, when I did recover, I decided to invite all the people I knew and had played with at the time to come, have a party in the house before we gave it up. Mother prepared a banquet starting with Atholl Brose, a great cauldron of it that went down very well and set the tongues wagging. They were an interesting lot. Fulton MacKay, Andrew Kerr, Gordon Jackson, 'Gibbie' and Gudrun Ure; a whole lot of them came to the party including Moultrie Kelsall, and it was good fun.

Much of my time was taken up with hiring and making costumes. I was given the money and detailed off to buy the furnishings for the sets for *Hedda Gabler* and all the other plays we put on at the Citizens in those days. I got rather good and interested in furnishings; I used to go to a lot of sales round about Stirling, where you got fine bargains.

One amazing woodcut I found in a Dunblane junkshop (see plate 15). It has remained with me, cherished for fifty years, and reads:

Donald McLeod of McLeod, chief of the Dunvegan clan
Served under five crowns –
King William, Queen Anne, George I, II, III
Walked to London from Skye when he was a hundred
And died at the age of one hundred and two

You could get a mahogany table for ten pounds or a birdcage for a shilling. Moultrie Kelsall suggested that I should have a shop in Dunblane. He would go in with it and supply some of the stock if I would supply the remainder of it.

So I went ahead and rented a little shop in a small street in Dunblane. At that time it was the main street; the road to Perth was not completed. This quaint little shop I called the Celtic Studio and fixed an awning over the window, in the continental style with blue and white stripes and scallops all round; very fetching. I bought some very interesting stuff and was doing well indeed, really. You could get bits of furniture for next to nothing at the sales, scrape them down to the natural wood; very fashionable at the time. But one day a nearby barracks full of Polish soldiers came hurling down the little narrow street with a great army lorry and bashed into my beautiful new awning, smashing it to smithereens.

All the Poles jumped out of this vehicle and rushed into the shop. They couldn't speak English, and they threw arms in the air, bowed and clicked their heels, tried to apologise. One of them had just enough English to say he would go and fetch an officer. And the officer happened to be Kazimier Rauszer; he, Kazik (pronounced Kasheek) came in, arranged to have the awning renewed and started to take a very keen interest in the stock in my shop. Then he began to come each day and buy something. I had a certain amount of jewellery and objects like brass lamps, all kinds of things. He bought a tiger skin and he bought a brooch. Another day it would be some other trinket; gradually I got interested in him because he seemed to have a great knowledge of period stuff, and was very, very interesting to talk to. He was also good-looking.

So I said to him one day, 'She's a very lucky girl that you're buying all these pieces of jewellery for. Might I ask who it is? Is it your wife or your girlfriend? Or who?'

And he said, 'Oh no, no, no. It is not. It is you yourself that I am buying these things for, I hope.' And of course that amused me no end. He then asked me if he could take me out, and so on, and we went for long walks around Dunblane. It was all very romantic. I became very much in love with him and he with me, and it was a beautiful romance.

Eventually, one day, as we had to cross a railway line, the express train was already due from Perth to Glasgow. Suddenly he grabbed a hold of me forcefully and said, 'Ronishau (which is my nickname) you cannot move from here till you say "yes, I will marry you"!'

Panic-stricken, more with joy and delight than fear, I promptly said, 'Yes!'

Life seemed to be accelerating, so much was happening at the one time. Morag and Nigel were packing to go off to New Zealand and they decided to take mother with them. My father had taken ill in the flat in Glasgow that my mother had retained throughout the War. Father then got pneumonia and died. His remains were taken back up to Skye where he was buried. My poor mother was so sad and so devastated she really felt she needed to make a change. She went with Morag and Nigel to New Zealand, sailed there in 1954. Mother wrote about the trip:

Dear Rhona wanted me to keep a diary and gave me this one to record what I remember of my early life. Here I am on the *Rangatiki* on my way to New Zealand to visit with Morag, Nigel and the dear children. It seems a long time since I was born on the Isle of Skye in 1884, seventy years ago. I left Skye in 1901 to come to my brother Duncan's wedding. Jimmy came with me. We joined the wedding party on the way to Arran. I first met my future husband going to the wedding. Eight years later we were married in Skye and had forty-five years of married bliss. Instead of returning to Skye after Duncan's wedding, I took a post in Glasgow with Ogg Brothers where I stayed until I went to Liverpool to keep house for my brother Duncan, while his wife, Belle, went to Arran till their daughter Ruby was born. I loved my stay in Liverpool and had a very happy time. I was with them when Màiri was born in Highton in 1904. My beloved father died in 1906 and I stayed at home with poor mother till I married in 1909. I then spent the happiest years of my life in Liverpool bringing up my five children, helped by the kindest husband in the world. I am absolutely lost without my darling Chris.

Morag and Nigel treated me to a trip to New Zealand and we sailed on 26 November from Tilbury. Rhona, Chris, June, Marianna and George all came to see us off.

It was a sad parting knowing it would be two years before we all got together again. I little thought when I left Skye that I would ever go to the end of the world, and now here I am in New Zealand after five weeks of sea trip. The *Rangatiki* ran into a terrific storm. We couldn't put the pilot ashore until we called at Nunacao. We went ashore there, and afterwards at Panola. We stopped to let the Pitcairn islanders on board with their beads, baskets and bananas.

Rhona wanted me to write the names of our ancestors. My father was Angus MacLeod, son of Neil, son of Duncan, son of Alan, son of Murdo. My mother was Rebecca MacKinnon, daughter of Donald MacKinnon and Catriona Finlayson. We are supposed to be of the Raasay MacLeods.

I am very impressed with New Zealand and consider it a great privilege to be able to come. Morag and Nigel treated me to this wonderful sea voyage and it has helped me such a lot to get over my loss. I miss my beloved Chris so much and feel so far from his resting place. Aunt Enid gave us a great welcome on arriving on New Year's Day and I found a Gaelic cable from dear Uncle Iain awaiting me and letters from my children. New Zealand is a very fine country. We arrived at Auckland in glorious weather and took sleepers to Wellington. Peter met the train in the early morning and motored us to Heratonga where Aunt Enid had a wonderful breakfast ready for us. The house they were promised in Wellington fell through. The owners sold it before we got here and it was wonderful of Aunt Enid to take such a large family into her dear wee house – seven of us including baby Duncan.

Morag and Nigel got busy house hunting and after

looking at many places decided to buy 176 Waterloo Road, Lower Hut, Wellington. It is a splendid house – garage, and a very lovely garden with flowers galore and beautiful shrubs and trees. It is only a few steps to the first school – Chillten St James – and they are very happy there. Quentin [their oldest son] has to go by bus to Wellesley College, Days Bay, and he comes back by train. We are within twenty minutes from Wellington, quite near the sea and the hills are a great delight. Wellington Harbour is very fine, surrounded by high hills with snug homes overlooking the harbour. It is growing and expanding very rapidly. The climate is very like our own in Skye – plenty of rain and cold winds. We are fortunate to arrive in the summer season; the weather is perfect. I love listening to the sheep bleating away on the hillside, dogs barking at them. It sounds for all the world like being in Upper Breakish at the time of shearing and dipping.

Ultima Thule

So Langarth had been given up. Before going to New Zealand, mother sold the house she and father had bought in Bute, and she bought another one in Skelmorlie down the Clyde. This one she shared with my sister June and her husband for some time. Then they gave that house up and nothing remained now but the flat in Glasgow, and the use of the house at Liveras, Skye.

Fortunately, before father died and mother went off to New Zealand, Kazik and I decided to get married. We were married in the Cathedral in Clyde Street, Glasgow, by Father Sydney McEwan, the singing priest (see plate 16). It was a wonderful wedding and we spent our honeymoon in Pitlochry and also in Bute. Then we came back to Glasgow to occupy the flat, although we had started our married life in the little gate lodge of Langarth, Stirling. The big house had been given up but we retained the little lodge for quite a while, and that was about the happiest time of my life.

Kazik had a lot of difficulty obtaining work as a scientist engineer and inventor. He wouldn't give up his Polish name or change it from 'von Rauszer'. He also wouldn't take British nationality, was proud of his own name and family in Poland and wished to remain a Pole, although he loved the British people as much as any of us and got on very well with everybody. It was hard going in those early days. Sometimes Kelvin Hughes would employ him and then he would do a spate with Scotts, the engineering company, and finally he ended up as a back-room boy in the Hoover company. Indeed, he was the inventor of the 'keymatic' washing machine pump system and was like his uncle before him, who invented the welding system for the world. He used to lie in his bath and invent all sorts of things.

Kazik had a very extravagant lifestyle, always smoked the very best cigarettes and thousands of them. And he liked his wine. Thank goodness he wasn't too keen on hard drinks, but he liked everything to be of the very best quality. His shoes, for instance, were the most expensive he could buy, although he didn't mind if his wardrobe was somewhat shabby. Corduroy trousers were worn till they were almost threadbare; his old tweed jackets he got very fond of and wouldn't give up; a couple of formal suits he hardly ever wore.

Laughter rang out round the table, the wine was good and we were mellow. The Tilley lamp hissed as it cast its weird glow from the top of the ceiling, shaping the outline of our features. The little room was above an antique shop, well, a crossing between that and a den in Montmartre. 'Little Paris in the heart of Glasgow,' Kazik called it (starting on the vodka).

'What about joke number seventeen?' More laughter.

'I hope you all realise you are on tape,' I shouted, shoving the beastly little tape recorder into the centre of the table, its brown discs rotating hypnotically.

'No, no, no,' laughed my niece hysterically, 'let's record silence instead.'

'Well, all right, let's 'ave 'ush. We will need a new tape for that,' I said. 'And we haven't got one.'

'Yes, we have,' said Kazik. 'You can use the one I had last Sunday, in the cave, when we all went birdwatching.'

Soon I found it, and fixed it carefully. Slowly it began to unwind, round and around . . . drip, drip, drip came the echoes from the cave. Then the most peculiar noises rose up from it: 'grian 's oonst . . . achair . . . iasg . . . ealasaid . . . uisge . . . uisge . . . u-u-u-isge'.*

Kazik jumped up from the table, 'Dhis is a phenomena,' he said, 'it's uncanny – incroiable. Dhese are voices from the past, from another world. I know. I have heard them before.'

Hurriedly I tried to put the thing off, but Kazik wouldn't let me. As an ardent searcher into psychic culture he was already making notes deciphering the disc at slow speed. It was uncanny, every time we put it on again we got more and more voices. All through the night we worked and just as dawn was breaking and the Tilley lamp had run dry, we played back on this weird and spooky tape, the story as it unwound itself to us . . .

Big tears rolled out of Grian's eyes, down to his chin and dropped from his chin to his shoulder, then trickled under his arms, sad, sad. He looked through the mouth of the cave and saw the tall, lean, scraggy, volcanic mountains. So little grew on them, soon the snows would come and there would be nothing green. He was hungry now – desperately hungry – he grabbed a piece of stone and flung it at Oonst. She would know what that would mean. She had a reserve of puinneags, small green sweet leaves. They grew under stones inside the cave. She lifted a large flat stone, her bosoms touching the cold surface of it as she plucked five or six of them and brought them to him. He raised himself on one elbow and she fed him the puinneags. Her black

* grian . . . uisge – the sun and lightness, distance, fish, Elizabeth, water

hair hung over his shoulder and fell down his back. When he'd finished eating she bit the side of his neck. He liked that, she knew it. Moving away from him, she picked up a flat shell and took it to the drip of water coming from a split in the stone of the cave – drip, drip, drip all the time. She brought it back to him and knelt beside him. He was already sitting up nibbling his toe-nails reflectively. From the corner of his eye he was watching Ealasaid, one of his women.

Oonst knew how he felt about Ealasaid and how Ealasaid felt about him. Ealasaid had as many children to him as she had fingers on one hand. They sat huddled around her now while she poked her toes under the rotten root of an old tree protruding from the mud floor, to scatter out the mice from under it. Through the slits of her greasy hair over her face you could see her eyes, vicious shining beads of hate. Oonst spat in her direction and threw some more wood on the fire, creating huge black smoke bodies on the wet walls. Then she danced to these shadows twisting and turning and tantalising, till Ealasaid could stand it no longer and determined to make a plan . . . a plan of destruction.

She would make three necklaces from teeth and stone for Oonst's three children, Achair, Each and Iasg, to bribe them to come with her to collect more shellfish on the sandy strip. The strip that the sea sometimes covered and sometimes left behind, according to the will of their God of the Moon.

Big Grian knew these women would kill for him, but he wondered how. Not that it mattered. He had too many mouths to feed anyhow, but he didn't want to part with Oonst. He had need of her always. He would swap Ealasaid for a hunk of horseflesh any day. She was now moving towards the mouth of the cave the rain slanting across it. When she came back she was carrying handfuls of stone and teeth, dug out from the refuse used to strengthen the walls of their home. Then squatting down in front of the steaming stone dish on the fire, she bit strands of sea kale into thin brown strips to thread the necklaces. When she'd finished, she sprang up, jumping up and down, spreading her nostrils and her eyes with her fingers to imitate monsters, she slapped her own five children, paralytic with fear, into a corner. Then quickly she lead Achair, Each and Iasg, the children of Oonst outside, dangling the necklaces she'd made before them as bait.

Then they ran and they ran naked across the strip of water till they reached the island, the island that came and went, exposed now with the water moving over the sand, like the grease oozing over the dish they cooked their food in. The gap between the strip and the land was filling, then being sucked back again like a spittle in the throat. If her plan worked, she would play and dance with the children here till the sea crept up on them; then being a sheep's carcass length higher than they were, she would run back to safety and leave them till the mighty waters came and covered them. She would beseech the Moon to draw the waters higher and higher than ever before. So she dug her knees into the wet sand and swung her arms, her head and her body round and round in the one direction. She stretched out her arms to reach the tentacles of light falling from the great swollen ink-fish face of the Moon. She had no pity now, even though they had all played there many times on that same strip, dancing and screeching, rolling and fighting in the hot sun, catching seagulls and eating them, feathers and all.

Once they'd seen a large creature from the sea spread out there. They had nearly sat on it, taking it for a rock, but then it moved and slithered back into the wide ocean; three of them could stand in the shape left behind by its foot.

Digging her nails in the sand and rubbing handfuls into her hair, she rose and stiffened her limbs and yelled, 'Swallow them, swallow them, and add the tears of Oonst to the waters of their destruction.' But little did she know the power of her petition. At the edge of her world a tidal wave had started. The Moon moved back to push it on through the skies that were torn and ravaged, lightning splitting them, across the once smooth sea the six men's high wall of water was driven towards them accompanied by the screeching of the Witches of the Wind.

Before her greasy black hair mingled with the seaweed and her pregnant body swelled, she had had time to think of Oonst, still lying in the arms of Grian, back in the bochan she would never see again. Drip, drip, drip. The terror without had not reached them yet. Oonst stretched out her hand for the long thin brown strip of kale and wound it around her long white fingers and spoke the murmurings of love into it, till suddenly the mouth of the cave yawned wide and belched forth all the waters of the mighty seas and the island that was, was no more . . .

The thin brown tape went spinning on, the tape that we would never use again . . . since we all know it has been used already. How, then, do you explain all this? We spent many nights trying to solve the strange phenomenon and looked to Kazik who was calm and unruffled by the whole experience.

'Well, I don't know,' he said. 'How can we know for certain? Dher is one thing, many times during the War I have had a glance into the past and also into the future. Dhis makes me think that all are one. The past, the present and the future. Dher is a short moment before falling asleep, when the mind develops a greater speed, a clearer brain. You see the whole globe at once, so to speak. Through strain and emancipation you can prolong dhis moment and if you, shall we say, murdered your body, your soul and your heart broaden; you are, how shall I say, holy, emaciated, partly in another world. We are like a gramophone disc with grooves, only our minds work at such a speed that it is only in time of great deprivation that we are able to slow down sufficiently to see into one of these grooves. It can be any one of them, depending on where the disc stops. Let me explain. Once when I was leading a party over the Pyrenees, it became necessary for us to spread out and I got lost, separated from the others. I must continue alone, no use to lie here on the frozen earth any longer. This was a rugged country of half burned trees and crushed stones. There was a path, yet not a path, and the land below was darkish. Near things seemed amplified, near yet far, going yet coming like in a dream, thirty-six hours climbing to no real purpose that I could remember.

'Keeping to the path that seemed to have had no beginning and would surely never end, I seemed to glide round a rock that tried to hide a valley, slowly the path was swallowed up in mist. Stone became water and I knew that I was descending in a shallow river, high rocks like banisters on either side tearing the flesh of my hands. Geographically displaced, I staggered on again finding once more the dirty, dusty track. Nothing surprised me, nothing was new. Then, suddenly, some clairvoyance of the brain told me that it was over, help was near. There were sounds like music going, and going in the wind; I felt my body, it was all there helping me on in oblivion. The sound of muffled bells disturbed me, the music of them wafting through the mist, a morning mist lifting slowly to reveal what looked like the first green grass ever, so wet and so fresh. Goats feeding off it that might have been there since the beginning of time. The only proof of human ownership were the blue-green patches on their skins and the persistent sound of bells. A chill ran through me. I felt as though I were taking part in a nativity play. As though God would speak to me . . . then an overwhelming awareness that I was not alone transfixed me. I felt a touch on my shoulder and twisted my eyes round painfully. A ray of light fell through the haze and outlined the figure of a man. A man too far away to have ever touched me. His feet were large in rough-hewn sandals. Slowly my body dissolved to the ground in a cold wet faint. It was too much. Then it was that the song came to me. A little ditty half in English and half in Spanish. As I regained consciousness the words repeated themselves over and over again. "Buttons on a blanket. Nadia lo ha visto* . . ."

'When I came to, there was a sharp pain in my eyes. Fearfully, I opened them against a persistent glinting and took in my surroundings – a dark candlelit cave sparkling with moisture like jewels – strips of amethyst glinting in the walls. Strange primitive paintings seemed to come alive. There was a strong smell of onion soup

* Nadia lo ha visto – nobody ever saw

and I was lying on a goatskin bed. Suddenly what seemed to be a large hairy animal moved towards me. As it got closer I was aware of a very tanned face topped with jet-black hair, like a hedgehog.

The mouth exploded into a smile of ten thousand teeth and a voice said, "I took the liberty, you looked as though you needed human care. My name is Gabriel Enamorado. Would you care for some soup?"

'I gulped down the first warm food I had had for many days with a feeling of beatitude, thawing out slowly and becoming more aware of the paintings on the walls, the ragged trousers and leather jacket of my benefactor; the tick, tick, ticking of what must have been a transmitting set or a drip. That feeling of "been-there-beforeness" still persisted. I asked my host if it was he who had been singing the little ditty. But he emphatically denied it.

'To cut a very long story short, Gabrielo Enamorado was a Spanish Republican and very well used to sheltering all kinds of fugitives. He was not at all surprised to find me and soon we were talking like old friends. In a few days he helped me to reach Pampelona.

'Two years later I found myself in Scotland where I had a chip of amethyst set in gold. I knew not why, as I had very little money, but perhaps it was an investment. Gold was safe and the beautiful translucent colour of this chip was rare. Not long afterwards I felt I must dispose of my amethyst and travelled up to Glasgow so to do. I searched for a reputable dealer, then came on a little antique shop that intrigued me. I lifted the latch and went in. There were candles burning on a little ormolu side table and right in the middle, the light flickering on it, was a twin amethyst to mine, an exact duplicate and a voice in the semi-darkness was chanting, "Buttons on a blanket.

Nadia lo ha visto . . ." My brain clouded over, the past became present. "Where did you hear that?" I said.

'I don't know,' said my wife. 'It's half English, half Spanish; I got it from my grandmother.'

'So you see, it is possible for the gramophone disc to revolve and for us to stick occasionally in the same groove. Carissamo. Who shall say?'

With not much money coming in as a newly married couple, I decided that I must find some work. As I was not qualified for anything at all, it wasn't easy to think what to do. I had been offered a job with a dry cleaning firm to do the window dressing for sixteen shops. So I converted part of the flat into a studio and was given a van and a driver. I went round these sixteen shops and cleared their windows out, then invented some sort of display to advertise the firm. Kazik was very helpful in this; I sometimes put windmills in their window and little rivers, all sorts of animated things, and we used what they called Sangamo machines to get rocking horses rocking and windmills turning.

Kazik longed for the sea, partly because he said that they'd only got the Vistula River in Poland. Most Poles had an urge to go to sea, from the famous Conrad onwards I suppose. So he took a notion to buy a boat and the opportunity arose when a ship came from Poland, the *Battery*. It had a number of ballet dancers on board and their object was to remain in this country. In the end they weren't allowed, and the ship had to go back to Poland, with all the ballet dancers.

But Kazik bought the small captain's cutter from the Polish *Battery*. It had no superstructure, no wheelhouse and no engine, and almost all its interior was missing. However, he bought the hull and had it transported by road to a large garage in Byres Road in Glasgow. We commenced work on it, not before truly christening it in style with a bottle of champagne, which we could ill afford at the time. We would do the proper christening at the launching on the Clyde when we had completed the work needing done on her. She would be called *Pythagoras*, Kazik's choice of course, and in my ignorance I called it 'Petigorus' because that was the way he pronounced it.

So we laboured and laboured, building a wheelhouse, installing a Penta engine, caulking and painting, anti-fouling, creating a galley and bunks, you name it; how we slaved! One day working away, a gentleman from the university walked into the garage. He was from Africa, a great big dark, swarthy fellow. And he said to Kazik, 'Please, can I assist you? I love nothing better in this world than caulking boats. My father had a boat in Africa and I just love to lie on my belly or lie on my back under a boat, I am never so happy.'

So Copey got to work. As he worked he sang like an angel; rather, very like Paul Robeson! And the work was getting done little by little; all the friends we had made fun of us, joked about us and helped as best they could. The great day arrived when she was to go by road, down to the Bowling Basin on the Clyde and be launched. What a day that was! Diligently we slogged away at that boat which soon became known to our friends as 'the ship that never went to sea'. We had lots of visits from Finlay J MacDonald; all sorts of people were anxious that we should get it on the water some day. They couldn't be as anxious as we were, but the trouble was we had no money, or very little left. So I had to do something about it.

Finlay J MacDonald, the Gaelic producer of the BBC, was a frequent visitor to us in the flat in Glasgow. He offered me a job, to launch a magazine called *Gairm* with him. But he had no money either, or so he said. He had acquired offices in Bath Street in Glasgow and wanted me to take the blank magazine, which didn't even have a cover on it, round to all

1. Mairianna Sykes with children Rhona, Christopher and Duncan

2. Mother Mairianna MacLeod, aged sixteen

3. Baby Rhona, 1911

4. The MacLeods of
Breakish, Skye, *c.*1910

5. Rhona, with mother, cousin Ruby and Skipper Gillespie
aboard *The Trident* at Kinloch, *c.*1920

6. Cousin Ruby's wedding at St Giles Cathedral, Edinburgh, 1924 (Rhona, far left)

7. Rhona painting the kilt for John Duncan MacRae, Citizen's Theatre, Germany, ENSA

8. Costume designer, Citizen's Theatre, Glasgow, 1947
(Rhona, bottom row right)

9. Rhona and Kazik working on *Pythagoras* with
Petroushka (Yorkshire terrier)

10. Citizen's Theatre, January 1947

11. Duncan MacLeod, Breakish (brother of Rhona's mother)

12. Skeabost House, Skye (home of Uncle Duncan in the 1920s)

13. Wren Sykes aboard A P Herbert's notorious
Water Gypsy, Thames, 1941

14. Breakish men, Flanders, World War I

15. Donald McLeod of McLeod, Dunvegan clan chief,
original woodcut

16. Marriage to Kazimier von Rauszer, with cousin Stanislaus
and sister June, Glasgow 1948

17. Rhona and Kazik
aboard *Pythagoras*

18. Original drawing by Rhona, self-portrait as Sophia Maria

19. Rhona's uncle John MacLeod, Broadford, World War I

20. Christopher Sykes (top row, far left) and the
Liverpool Sports Club, *c.*1911

21. Rhona (second from left) on the ferry to Skye
with sister Morag

22. Rhona at home, 2004

23. Portrait of Rhona, aged 12, by Frank T Copnall, 1923

24. Original painting by Rhona, 'Working the Peats', 1972

"Hey" Vatsic, There's a King and Queen Wanting Tea.'

25. Original sketch by Rhona, 'Hey Vatsik,
there's a King and Queen wanting tea!'

the businesses, shops and places that I knew, get as many of the pages filled in with advertisements as I could.

I agreed to have a shot at this and went round to Coplands, the shop which had once been called Ogg Brothers, where my mother had made her start. I asked to see the manager and he very kindly saw me. I told him the story of my mother, how his grandfather had given her her first job, then told him about this magazine which Finlay J was starting. He gave me my first advertisement. I must have contacted every shop in Glasgow: I even went to William Morris and bargained, said we would give him free advertising in our magazine. It would be a Highland magazine, mostly in Gaelic, reach all the Outer Islands and abroad, and would be very good for him to have his advertisements in it. We would do that in exchange (I don't know how I had the cheek) for his furnishing the offices in Bath Street with a desk, table, chair, safe and necessary things, filing cabinets and so on.

Funnily enough, this he agreed to do, so we had a very posh office! And then Finlay was struck with an idea for the front page of the magazine. So Kazik suggested, 'Why not have a cockerel on it, since it is called *Gairm* and Polish cockerels are very beautiful indeed.' So we contacted a Polish friend of Kazik's who designed and painted the cover for the magazine. It is still going as a publication today, though I got nothing for my part in it, or any money. So I left at the first opportunity to go to Edinburgh, to design the costumes and sets for a nativity play written and produced by Robert Kemp.

I had hoped that he'd give me the part of the Virgin Mary, but no such luck. Kazik at the time was designing something for Babcock & Wilcox, so I got him to design the wings for the Angel Gabriel. He wasn't too keen, especially when I wanted them to be at least six feet tall and made of translucent perspex. Not an easy job at all, but he did it and they were exquisitely beautiful. The trouble was, he would have to bring them through from Glasgow to Edinburgh. He tried going on a bus with them but was soon sent off. So the alternative was a train. He managed that, but coming out of the station in Edinburgh there was a howling gale; he must have looked ridiculous wandering along the road to the theatre. Naturally he couldn't get into a taxi with these enormous perspex angel's wings fluttering under his arms.

After Christmas, back to the boat with a little bit more money in hand. Moultrie Kelsall was very good at throwing the odd drama programme at me, giving me snippets in quite a few radio plays: *The Trial of Madeline Smith* for one and *The Window in Thrums* another. But for *The Window in Thrums* he persuaded me to learn the Forfar dialect that I knew nothing about. However, I thought it worth my while to go through to Forfar to try to learn it. This was a big mistake.

I thought the best way was to get a job, so I went to the Labour Exchange and asked them if they'd got anything I could do. I told them why I wanted to spend a few days learning the dialect, and they sent me to the forestry. It was the hardest job I ever undertook in my life, and I was mortified at what these women had to endure.

Our job, after the trees were felled, was to lift six-foot, four-foot and three-foot tall logs off the ground, place them on our bellies, lean them against our chests and shoulders, and carry them to a measuring post. We stood them against the measuring post, then lazy louts of men would come along on tractors or motorised machines, place them on their machines and motor them away. I endured this for one whole day. My hands were bleeding, there was resin stuck under my nails, I thought I would never be able to clean up my skin again, and I went to the office and resigned – never again! I got back to the hotel and steeped myself in a hot bath for hours, aching all over.

Ultima Thule

So I went back to the Labour Exchange and told them that this had been a lousy job, would they give me a much easier one, please! So, they sent me to an egg-sorting factory. That was quite good fun – you just sat on your bahookey and the eggs were passed on a sort of belt through a machine which exposed the insides – you picked out the eggs that had embryos. An easy job, I stuck that for about a week; then went back to Glasgow only to find that *The Window in Thrums* by J M Barrie had already gone out on the air – I'd missed it!

However, I got several other small snippets in radio plays, mostly produced by A P Lee and Moultrie Kelsall. One day we were doing a play about the Clearances and I was a young girl. The Redcoats came into our cottage and were going to abuse me. I was supposed to scream as loud as I could but it so happened I had a sore throat and I could hardly scream at all, so Moultrie Kelsall said to Crampsey and one of the other men, 'Just lift her up and fling her against the wall!' This they did and my posterior went right through the plaster facing. They drew a circle round the mark for posterity. At least I did scream – nearly took the studio roof off!

When the last of the brass screws were sunk and counter-sunk, the caulking all done and everything shipshape, we got very depressed because we just did not have quite enough money to get *Pythagoras* launched. She had to be taken by road and it would be an expensive business getting her down onto the Clyde. So, having accumulated a lot of furniture in my mother's flat, leftovers from the shop in Dunblane, I decided to have a private sale. I got hold of an antique dealer and told him to have a look at my stuff. He came, and I found myself selling bits of furniture that were very precious, an Irish bogwood altar with angels, a beautiful oak settle with Byzantine carvings on the panels, a spinet piano and many things I wasn't getting nearly the right price for.

However, we managed to get enough to pay the lorry drivers and people who were going to take the boat down to the Clyde. Fortunately, my brother Christopher had bought a house in the village of Bowling, and there was a basin where we would keep our boat. So, we had a wonderful party up in Christopher's house. We got together, had a bottle of champagne and cakes, fun, music and laughter; a very grand affair. His house was overlooking the Clyde and we could see the big ships passing with their flickering lights at night. We were looking forward to living for a spell on our own boat. I can truthfully say this was the most magical time of my life – to live on a boat and get up in the early morning, look through the hatch and comb your hair. Mine was very long; I would comb it out, the seagulls would swoop down, collect my bits of hair flung in the air and sweep off again.

It was really romantic. Kazik and I were very much in love and we had a darling little Yorkshire terrier called Petroushka (see plate 9). I used to go up to the Citizens Theatre in the daytime and they allowed me to be wardrobe mistress for a spell. So I would be sewing and making costumes for the various plays we would put on in exchange for having small parts in each and all of them. And so it went on.

But before the launching, while Kazik's work table, vice and tools were all still in the garage where we kept the boat, I decided to get a hunk of wood and try to do a carving of my beloved husband's face. He had such wonderful high cheek-bones, a lovely bone structure altogether. So I laboured at this hunk of wood; I had chosen a very hard piece and chiselled and chiselled, eventually managing to get a resemblance. I was so moved with the likeness that my tears began to flow and Kazik came in, caught me at it and said, 'Mechelka (that was his nickname for me, it means 'little shell' in Polish), Mechelka, stop crying because when I am dead and you have this likeness hanging up on the wall you will see that tears will flow from it.' Of course I thought he was havering and took no notice really, blew my nose, snuffled my tears away. But it was true, later on this did happen.

It had been a happy, sunny day when finally our beloved boat took to the water. Both the keepers were there and quite a lot of strangers were hanging about; a second bottle of champagne was cracked on the hull by my younger sister Cairistiona, known as June. We all stepped aboard. June had brought a lovely cake with little miniature ships all over; we ate that, drank the champagne and were as happy as sandboys.

Then June and her two little children went back up to Glasgow and left Kazik and I on board our own boat; sitting on our own bunk, wondering if it would sink beneath us, or if we would risk staying the night on her. We decided on the latter and snuggled into a double bunk with a little gimbal lamp shining beside us, exhausted and happy, but so tired. We slept and slept and in the morning I stretched my arms out – one of them hung out of the side of the bunk – and to my astonishment it was soaking wet. The bilges were full, the water was up to the edge of our mattress and in great panic we paddled out of bed and started pumping like all hell to get rid of the water – we thought we'd sink at any minute! But around Bowling Basin in those days there were about six other boats of various descriptions, from magnificent yachts to little boats. There was a tremendous camaraderie and before you could say 'Jack Robinson' they were all round us helping to pump out the water and put things to right on board our boat. The lock keepers were excellent too and Kazik discovered where the trouble lay; it was rectified.

We decided that we couldn't really leave her, so we stayed on for another week and then decided it was high time we had a proper bath, because we only had washing facilities on board. We had small heads (lavatories) and all the necessary things, a charming little wood stove, comfortable and extremely warm, just a wonderful little nest we so much enjoyed. But it was better that we should go up to my brother's house and have a good steep in a bath. Then we discovered public baths not far away with a swimming pool, sauna and the lot. I decided to investigate.

I was astonished at this establishment – there were bathrooms up a flight of stairs, huge Victorian mirrors, gigantic baths with brass taps and fittings, all glittering and shining. It was immaculately clean. Some of these baths and public conveniences in Scotland are fine examples of Victorian grandeur, far superior to anything that is built today. But I couldn't help thinking of a funny story I had heard in Skye where most people in my day were very earthy and nearly all had a sense of humour.

So there was an old boy who decided to leave Skye and go to Glasgow with his pal. They went by car and got as far as these baths I'm now talking about. Donald said, 'I'm afraid I need to go somewhere, I need to relieve myself.'

And his pal said, 'Well, you'd better go in there.'

So Donald was reluctant at first and said, 'Well, here, no, I can't very well go in there.'

And his pal said, 'On you go, I'll wait for you, on you go!'

And so Donald went in, climbed the stairs and went up. There were mirrors and padded seats and chairs, steam baths and goodness knows what all! He came rushing out again and his friend said, 'Well, Donald did you do it?'

'Oh no,' said Donald, 'I just couldn't do it there. I felt so shabby.'

'Oh dear me,' said his friend, 'I'm afraid we won't find any peat stacks here in Glasgow for you to do it.'

Life with Kazik was truly an adventure . . .

The moon was full and filling the forecastle with light. Too much light, Kazik said, it kept him awake. Liar! He'd been snoring his head off for the past couple of hours. But, indeed, there was something eerie about tonight all the same. Our boat, which we loved and lived in, and had made ourselves from the gunwales up, seemed to be warning us. She was behaving strangely, her fenders squeaked and squawked like banshees against her hull and the Tilley lamp started to peter out noisily in the midships where the main hatch was open to the sky.

Had Kazik said his prayers? I doubted it. Had I said mine? No. It was strange how our two so different religions had merged together in the fifteen years of our married life. Kazik, a staunch Polish Catholic and me, half wee Free, half Church of England.

Kazik began to snore again so I would just pray for both of us. But even this only comforted me a little, the queer noises continued and my pulse began to bang a bit. There was something moving on deck. Sure, seagulls? Rats perhaps? Oh no . . . I cuddled closer to Kazik. I would not waken him. He slept like a log and needed it.

Suddenly there was a noise like someone coming down the ladder from the hatch. I coughed, deliberately, and reached for the little knife a Norwegian sailor had given me last summer as a souvenir. I lay rigid and waited, watching the moon's rays flickering on the knife.

Then a man's gruff voice said, 'Is the skipper aboard?'

Quickly I plonked my hand over Kazik's mouth and I answered, 'Yes, what do you want?'

With that the footsteps came nearer and just as he was entering our cabin – no doubt thinking me alone – Kazik leapt at him in the dark and pinned him down. He would have squeezed the daylights out of him in his half wakened state, imagining himself back in the Resistance Movement. But the man managed to gurgle that he had been sent by the harbour master with a message.

'What, at four in the morning?' says Kazik.

'Aye, you're to shift your berth,' says the man. 'There's a fishing boat coming in here right now. I thought I'd give you warning so you could get yer things on and slacken off yer lines. I'm going up to the village later on and can bring you back rolls and milk for your breakfast.'

'You can tell the harbour master to go to hell!' said Kazik. 'I'm not shifting out of here even for *The Queen Mary*. Harbour, harbour master did you say? Dher is no harbour master here on the canal, only the lock keepers, and I'm bloody sure I'm not shifting for them. You're lying,' said Kazik, gripping him again.

'No, no, sir,' squeaked the man, 'come and see for yourself! I'll wait on deck while you get your trousers on and take you along to the custom-house.'

Kazik suddenly became conscious of his bare feet and pyjamas. He couldn't go to the custom-house like that. 'Right then,' he said, 'we'll do just that.' This was the big mistake. While Kazik threw himself into his trousers using words like 'cholera' and 'merde' in rapid succession, our visitor had nipped on deck and completely disappeared.

In the morning all the boats had a visit from the local police. The description of the man they were looking for tallied exactly with our intruder. Moreover, no other fishing boat intended to take our berth and the papers that evening said that a boy had been murdered in a doctor's disused surgery only a few miles away, and the murderer was still at large.

'Is the skipper aboard?' he had said. 'Oh yes,' said I, 'what do you want?'

During our time on board *Pythagoras* we made many lasting friends and there was really no need for us to go to sea with our boat at all; no sooner did you put your nose out of the hatch and get onto the deck, than somebody would be shouting across to you, 'Hello there, could you possibly come with us to Ireland to Tournadee?', or 'Could you possibly come with us, we're going to sail up the Strangford River and we need crew.' We found ourselves crewing for every boat in the Basin and made some wonderful trips. We went to Orkney, Shetland and Ireland, all around the Clyde and Rothesay, when we lived aboard *Pythagoras* in Bowling Basin (see plate 17).

The following three stories from our cruises I wrote for radio broadcast, but only the first one, 'Finding's Keeping' was accepted.

You can visit the Orkney Islands by plane nowadays and (soon) by hovercraft, no doubt; that is, if you have a mind to it. And if you are not as blind as a worn commercial traveller you cannot fail to be bewitched by the fair fringe or periphery of the world. It was my good fortune a few years back, to sail there in an Orkney-built fishing boat, a boat that knew its own way home. And so it was, there came to my ears a story that is very hush-hush.

It concerns a couple of lads, deep-sea fishermen; they were from the Shetland Isles, and they chanced one night, going out to do a bit of flat-fish poaching for a change. There is a pretty heavy fine on it as you probably know, so they had to take great care, moving as silently as possible, without navigation lights among the islands and along Cliff Sound, nearly as far as Fitful Head. Without much of a catch, they decided to pack it in and lift their boards for the last time. It was then that they found their gear had got entangled with something most peculiar. They had an awful struggle getting it up, at first they thought it might be a bomb or a mine, or, 'damn it all, maybe a depth charge'? So, needless to say, they were very frightened indeed when they finally got the object on board. At first they were going to throw it back, but they got cold feet, in case it would explode, so they made way at a hell of a lick, a good six knots; a lot for them as she was an old boat with a dickey engine, but fortunately the tide was favourable.

They hadn't the nerve to even look at their catch till they were passing between Oxen Papa and Greenholm on their way into Scalloway, their home port . . . And my gosh, imagine their surprise when they found they had raised up what looked like a slipper box, a sort of decorated keisht (box). When they finally levered open its old rusted hinges, they couldn't believe their eyes . . . there was a shower of necklaces, and heaven knows how many jewels and coins! All I can say is thank goodness they found it after the Saint Ninian's Treasure was discovered because, believe you me, these young Shetland buccaneers don't want to part with it! Not for all the

Ross' Tea in Edinburgh. And naturally enough I am sworn to secrecy.

*　*　*

It was with a sense of high adventure that we entered Loch Ness on our return cruise from the Orkney Islands. We had been lucky, too, considering we were in a very old forty-three foot fishing ketch and the Pentland (Firth) had been kind to us, more than we deserved; the horrible vortexes had not swallowed us up as I feared they would, and we had made good time with sufficient visibility to see the Castle of May, John o' Groats and Lybster, and all those enchanting misty caves and inlets skirting the Caithness coast like lace around a semmet. Our holiday time was drawing to a close, and one of the crew (my husband) had had to take the Orcadian steamer *St Olaf* and catch a train to Glasgow. He was already several days adrift from his work. However, we, the remaining crew, the skipper, young John and myself were more fortunate; we had three more days remaining. The weather was fine and we intended to make the most of Loch Ness and the Cally (Caledonian Canal). I was particularly excited as I was dying to meet that daddy of them all, the Loch Ness Monster. I fully believed in him, so many reliable people had given me first hand accounts of terrifying encounters.

Why, there was the minister from Skye motoring home with his wife when suddenly the road was blocked by a heaving, vibrating monster making its way back into the loch. And even in my grandmother's time, there were tales of deer and sheep being swallowed alive by this elusive, multi-humped monstrosity.

So no wonder the tension was high, what with me at the wheel deviating more and more frequently towards floating branches . . . with humps on them, and marking buoys with heads, and our good friend Gerald the Skipper yelling his head off for me to keep on course, while he gave himself a shave before getting to the first lock at Fort Augustus. 'Where's that boy John? . . . give him the wheel, for God's sake or you'll have us all piled up on the starboard shore.'

But poor John was busy imitating a Maori war dance, or a Highland fling, while he frantically slapped his chest, his back, arms and thighs in an endeavour to smite the battalions of midges accumulating in the holes of his string vest, his ears and his eyelids. He had never experienced anything like it, nor had I; the wheelhouse windows were thick with them, only, being a Highlander from the Misty Isle* they didn't like the taste of my blood . . . they were far too used to it. When we tied up alongside the first lock at Fort Augustus, we were weary and bedraggled and I was furious that I had not seen sight nor sound of the Monster.

It did not take us long, however, to sprint up to the nearest hotel for a bath and a well-earned dram. The hotel we chose was a smart one with a well appointed bar; Gerald made straight for it, with John at heel. I slunk into a warm seat by the fire where I could observe the follies of men, and accept gracefully their attentions. It was then that I noticed the barman . . . or rather his ears (that was the first thing).

They seemed enormous and were completely pointed; they fascinated me, I couldn't stop looking. He must

* the Misty Isle – Eilean a'Cheò is the Isle of Skye's mainland name

have sensed this and fixed me with a penetrating gaze. The rest of his appearance fell gradually into place. He was tall, swarthy and aggressively good-looking, his movements stealthy and catlike. He was fascinating, yet at the same time acutely repellent . . . I sighed with relief when Gerald arrived with our drinks, breaking the hypnotic spell. Soon I excused myself saying, 'I must go back to the boat to prepare our supper.' I felt strangely uneasy and afraid to look again in the direction of the bar.

'Wait a jiffy,' Gerald said, 'I'll get a couple of bottles to take aboard with us.'

'No, no,' I protested, but it was too late. Gerald was talking volubly with the barman again, 'If you're too busy to get them just now, bring them down to the boat when you come off duty. You know where we are moored,' he bellowed, 'and bring your girl-friend too if you've got one.' Gerald was always like that; he hated to drink alone, and John had no stomach for it.

I trembled with unreasonable fear as I tried to prepare our supper in the little galley that night, and kept popping my head through the hatch, curiosity subduing fear like a mouse with a mousetrap. It was gone nine o'clock when he finally came . . . alone. He dumped two bottles of Bullochlade (Skye family whisky) on the table, and sat on the opposite bunk.

'I don't believe I know your name,' said Gerald. 'Do you take it neat?'

'I have no name,' said the stranger, 'and I loathe water.'

Gerald laughed, 'Well, what do we call you then?'

'You don't. I don't have a name, a country or a soul.'

'You must have a soul,' I said (rather piously) and could have bitten off my tongue.

'No,' he said, 'I sold it.'

'To whom?' said I.

'To the devil, of course. You do believe me,' he said, 'don't you?' and fixed me with his burning eyes.

'I do not.'

'Oh, yes you do, and I can prove it.'

'How?'

'You can meet me alone in the woods half a mile from here . . . at midnight. I will build a fire by the blighted holly tree, I will then draw the blood of an owl and mingle it with yours . . . and you will then see all, know all and forever be in my power.'

Indeed, it seemed I was already in his power . . . had been from the first moment I set eyes on him.

'You married by any chance?' asked John.

'Once, in Rumania,' said the man.

'Where is she?'

'Dead,' said the man, 'a climbing accident.'

'Did she fall or was she pushed?' asked John.

'Pushed.'

'Then, you must be a devil, right enough, and you had better get to Hell out of here straightaway, before you cast a buidseach on this boat, and ruin what's left of our cruise . . .'

'Now, take it easy, man,' said Gerald. 'If you want to argue, go out on deck.'

'Not a bad idea,' said John, and I had never seen him looking so angry. So the party broke up before it had begun, you might say, and I turned in to my bunk.

It was near twelve o'clock when I suddenly woke up in a state of terror. I wanted to move my limbs . . . rise up but I found I couldn't budge . . . I was paralysed. I could hear a great splashing noise round the boat. The wind had surely risen. I wanted to climb through my hatch, to investigate, but I found I could not move a muscle . . . Suddenly the boat listed a little, enabling me to see through the porthole. We were moored to a little jetty, and standing on it was the man with the pointed ears. As I watched, his bulk began to swell up and his neck to rear . . . his legs formed into an enormous tail . . . and raising what now seemed like fins, he soared upwards and then slithered his great body over the edge of the pier, and down, down, into the water.

I could not scream, I could not yell; I could only watch the two great humps move further and further away with the slithering tail in their wake. And now I know that I know, and have met, the Loch Ness Monster.

* * *

Deciding what to take in the way of clothes and victuals on a trip to the Isle of Skye is not easy. Do you leave the Clyde in a heatwave and arrive in a snowstorm? Or vice versa? Take bikinis or balaclavas? Anyway, you can guess for yourselves just how much a forty-two foot ketch will accommodate, not including normal ballast, the men's gear, etcetera, etcetera (as the Highlanders would say – especially the ones with lazy minds like myself). So let's get on with the trip. Here again, it doesn't do to use too much intelligence or imagination. Reserve everything you've got for the perils of the sea itself; besides, there is a handy wee book called *Clyde Cruising Club Directions*, including in its pages a clear description of all the hazards you might meet between here and the Isle of Mist.

Six a.m. is a rotten time to start for anywhere, but we had to be through the lock gates at Bowling to catch the tide – 'time and tide wait for no man' – so there wasn't a hope in hell of it waiting for me – a woman. Ralph, my husband* (he's a middling fair sailor) was coming too, of course, and Bertram – he's the skipper-owner and very well-off. We took along a young lad called John mostly for muscle. So that was the crew – 'three men in a boat' and me.

By mid-morning the weather was sweltering. We decided to put in at Rothesay, Bute, for a laugh more than anything, to mix for a while among the well-kent faces of those who, like ourselves, are part of the flotsam of the Clyde.

Then up the Kyles past Tighnabruaich, leaving Ardlamont Point and reaching Scate Island by nine. Next day we started to go through the Crinan Canal, lock after lock and more and more beauty, the banks dripping with flowers. One expects to run into the Lady of Shallot at the next bend. There are little J M Barrie islands in small lakes, and the lock keepers' cottages, some white with purple clematis growing up the walls. The not-so-distant mountains, stark and edgy in the setting sun, seem to be protecting them.

By the time we started blasting the horn for the last two locks, my arms and the backs of my knees were aching. Who would like to be bow-hooky through seventeen locks, and on galley duty at the same time? You try to throw a rope, or line (big enough to hold a liner) up a ten-foot wall. Naturally, you miss, and it comes back at you covered in green slime. The skipper

* Ralph, my husband – a by-name used for Kazik

swears at you, forgetting you're a lady, and when you are finally made fast you suddenly remember you've left a pan of bacon and bangers sizzling on the stove, and by the time you chisel off the bacon, slam it in a sandwich and stagger through the hatch with it you find you're at another lock, and John has left the stern line to help the 205-year-old lock keeper at the gates. So you throw the stern line yourself, then you leap for'ad to the bowline and heave on it to keep her from swinging out, your acrylic jackets on your two front teeth creaking with the strain. Sometimes we're on the mud, then we're off it again, minus a boat-hook.

'Hold hard, there's a boat coming through! We have to give it right of way . . . might be Prince Philip, perhaps?' Coil the ropes. Stow the buckets. Well, well, here she comes! All that fuss for an old crate (a dirty old barge) called *Blossom* (bless 'er). But wait till you see the luxury yachts when you reach the basin at Crinan, and the smart groups of sailing connoisseurs waiting to see what kind of a muck you make of your entrance! It's worse than a command performance – not like Rothesay with its teddy boys shouting, 'I'll gie ye two pounds for your bo-at, mister, and I'll make it a fiver if ye throw in the wifie stan'in' at the blunt end!' (That was me.) No indeed, at Crinan we were invited to make fast to an ex-RNLI (Royal Naval) boat by a character with 'RN' written all over him, his navy-blue shorts secured by a lanyard, his chest heaved up under a starched white shirt. He managed to indicate through a breathless giggle that coffee was in fact already made for us if we cared to come aboard.

Later that night I changed into a brown linen shift and tortoiseshell earrings, and tishied ashore on the arm of my husband. The hotel was just beginning to fill up and our navy boyfriend joined us for a beer. Bertram (our skipper) learned from him that he was 'not doing anything just now'. Berty calls a spade a spade.

'Oot o' work, are ye?' says he. 'Well, ye can sell fish for me from Scalloway in Shetland, I'll make you a good offer . . .'

Our little navy friend was horrified. He tried hard to cover up by quickly proclaiming he had once been a bartender for a week in Kuala Lumpar, or somewhere. 'Couldn't make a go of it, old boy.'

Bert was disgusted, and proceeded to feed potato crisps to a two-month old baby left at the next table, abandoned by its parents. When they returned they assured us it was quite all right, the baby really brought itself up. It was an experiment, you see. The father was a doctor. Bert asked them if they cared to come aboard. They did. The mother asked if she might put the baby on my bunk.

'But certainly . . .' I said. When she kicked off her shoes and clambered in beside it and started to breast-feed him I could hardly believe my eyes . . . I half wondered what he'd get – whisky, gin or beer – but all told it was a good party.

It must have been, for the next morning we felt ourselves gliding through the basin. We were on tow. I put my head through the hatch to investigate. The navy type had our bowline still made fast to his stern post, and was going out to sea.

When I yelled to him he suddenly slipped our line, his wash threw us right up against a beautifully painted powder-blue hull of another yacht. The owner bobbed up in his pyjamas as I was frantically trying to place a fend-off between our bowsprit and his wheelhouse windows. Whew! The language. Were we glad to be going out through the Dorist Mór* that day, out to the open sea and as far away as possible from Crinan.

I made a nest of a coil of rope, snuggled into it, slept and slept. I was not on galley that day and had VIP treatment, so I got suspicious. Probably they would all go ashore to the Mishnish Hotel when we got to Tobermory and leave me in charge of the boat. Well, I was dead right – that's just what they did do. I sat on deck, and with half-closed eyes watched the kaleidoscopic changes of colour – the blue, orange, green and red of the boats – this playground for sailors and seagulls, the beloved Tobermory. As we were making an early start in the morning I wouldn't have time to go ashore then either. Putting my shorts on again (and little else), I looked in the tiny mirror in the heads. It had a pattern on it like Spanish lace from sea corrosion. My face, reflected in it, seemed so very dark. Was I perhaps reincarnated? Had I risen up from the depths of these waters out of a skeleton galleon? No one would believe this was a British tan.

Mind you, the heat of the day was causing a deep haze when we were out at sea. It was not easy to make out landmarks, and beyond Ardnamurchan Point things got tricky. It was my watch. I should be sighting Muck, Eigg or Rhum on the port hand side. Bert had given me the compass course all right, but I couldn't help feeling I had gone off it somewhere. Then we saw Rhum, and Ralph took a bearing. We were miles off. God knows where I would have landed them. But we came back on course

* the Dorist Mór – the big door, end of the canal

towards the close of a perfect afternoon, and eventually sighted Sleat Point, its outline silhouetted on a shiny cucumber-green sea.

There was much to do when we got to Mallaig, apart from swapping drams for fish with the fishermen. The rigging had slackened, causing the mast to shoogle. Ralph tightened up the bottle screws and we took on stores. Next day, we left Mallaig with a cargo of kippers and a couple of immense cod. I decapitated them with numb hands while going through the whirlpools in the narrows of Kylerhea. The weather had changed completely. It was now bitterly cold. Have you ever tried scraping and gutting fish at sea, throwing the guts over the side when you feel you could throw your own guts over with far better speed and accuracy? So it was with me. The decks were awash into the bargain. I slithered about like a Glasgow drunk on a Saturday night.

We put in at Kyleakin on Skye without much palaver, having introduced myself in now half-forgotten Gaelic as 'nighean Mairianna Beathag' (the daughter of my mother and grandmother). It's customary to hand out a sort of family tree, which acts like a magic wand. You're on VIP treatment all the way. We supped afternoon tea with a couple of wee Free ministers at my cousin's hotel on the pier – like myself she is married with a Pole who has built a bochan on the pier into a new prosperous business, catering for a thousand or so cars and buses passing on and off the island in the season. Vatzik would clap his hands together with child-like glee, explaining 'that he only had to open the windows and fish the tourists in like haddocks . . . English, French, Russian, blacks and whites'.

We could only stay for one hour at the crumbling pier

at Broadford – long enough for me to leave a large hunk of my heart. The house we once lived in stood empty, the sun glinting on its windows, looking like tears. Then off we sailed past the islands of Scalpay and Raasay, and found ourselves in Portree harbour at ten o'clock that night dropping the hook alongside *Bluebottle*. Prince Philip himself was not aboard. We would have liked to have had a keek at him.

We rowed ashore and gave my sister Morag a ring from the rather smelly call box on the pier. After dressing for shore-going, next day – I felt very Compton MacKenzie-ish in my cape and gillie shoes – we were given an excellent lunch with a special wine in a house now run as an hotel, where I had spent a part of my childhood. Afterwards I took Ralph's hand and led him down towards the river. I would show him all the magic places. Crossing the suspension bridge, which I shoogled for old time's sake, we rather astonished a French lady guest trying to entice an elusive salmon. Ralph's Polish French came in very useful. He was able to explain exactly which rock it was hiding under. Her eyes showed faith in his judgment and childlike gratitude which endeared her to him, as only a French woman could, for the rest of the summer.

I hurtled him off speedily to see the ancient burial ground in the middle of the river, and the Crusaders' graves, and deliberately guided him through beds and beds of nettles, wishing he wore the kilt so that he would get stung to death. When we later motored back to Portree to rejoin the boat, who should we see, waiting to give us a farewell wave from the quayside but Madame Sombrere herself! So, when we set off again to make the passage round the north wing of Skye, it may have been my black mood – not the weather – that made everything seem so phantom-like. The gigantic Kilt Rock and Duntulm Castle – the very name 'Duntulm' filled me with a sinister sort of dread. I was secretly afraid we might sail right into those dreaded volcanic rocks (you had to keep fairly close in to land as the outlying small islands were an even greater hazard).

It was ten o'clock when we got into the shelter of Uig Bay, and I was mighty relieved and pleased to see my other little widowed sister who had fled from the big cities with her two sons and small daughter when her husband died. The end of her croft and the sea shingle merged. And there they all were, shining torches and swinging lanterns, the welcoming light mixing with the already effervescent waters . . . while we threw the lead to determine the depths, and dropped anchor.

I stuffed a bottle of whisky in my old sealskin bag, and, with a cargo of kippers from Mallaig we rowed ashore. The atmosphere of the cottage was heavenly after the boat – wood fires, hot soup and more whisky. Relations and friends dropped in, all in grand céilidh fettle – what a night!

Our skipper was supposed to be a confirmed bachelor . . . Were we mistaken, then, or had our bold Bertram really fallen lock, stock and barrel (mostly barrel) for my little widowed sister? Stories and songs were unlimited as the night wore on. Ralph and I would sleep ashore – it was all right for us! The skipper and John would return to the boat. But dear old Berty would not budge without the little widow whose future he had already planned. The children were no deterrent. He insisted on tucking them all in bed and patting each curly head paternally before rowing their mother, Ralph and

John off to the boat for another wee snifter. (After they'd gone I curled up and died.)

Meanwhile, out at the boat, Berty had turned on sweet music (interrupted spasmodically by the late night fishing forecast). The widow, however, being a sensible lass, decided to part from her newfound suitor and return home to her bairns before the Sabbath Day would fully dawn. Ralph rowed her ashore, promising to return with the dinghy – a promise he had no intention of keeping till the following day. They were bringing me a strupag (Gaelic, for tea) around five in the morning, when suddenly we heard the most unholy splashing and shouting.

Ralph flung on his wellington boots over his pyjama trousers and ran down to the shore to investigate. Apparently, my bold Berty had decided to follow the widow ashore, and having no dinghy, had launched the inflatable raft without inflating it. Consequently, the moment he got in, it collapsed and enveloped him; but, being a stubborn sort of chap, who likes to get his own way he managed to swim ashore, pushing the rubber raft ahead of him and calling – not for help – but sympathy and understanding from the little widow, sounding for all the world like a love-sick seal crooning for its mate. He then proceeded to lumber up the path festooned with seaweed and squelching with water. Finally Ralph persuaded him to postpone his ardent pursuit till the morning and return to the boat 'like a good fellow' – this time in the dinghy.

After that episode, further sailing was postponed for at least a couple of days, days of peaceful bliss when life was young again, and the world smelt of kindly things like bog myrtle, seaweed and smouldering wood and peat.

Bertram was once more in pursuit of the little widow, but without much success. He insisted on buying a side of mutton when he ran into her in the butcher's shop (for the children), but sad as it seems, dear Uncle Berty (as he was now nicknamed) was to get the brush-off, and, like a ship that passes in the night we unanchored and left – left Uig as it now was, but would never be again. Apart from us, the new ferry would see to that, the ferry from North Uist. They were already working on the old pier (visited by King Edward VIII), preparing for the thousands of strangers who might or might not be welcome.

With the forecast predicting stormy weather we couldn't risk taking a different course home. Anyway, we could see more clearly Idrigill Point in the morning light, with its hole in the middle like a darning needle, and the small islands, like children's bricks disordered and kicked about. Towards eleven, the wind got up and the fine rain turned to a flogging deluge, leaving deep potholes in the sea. Making round the back of Scalpay, I dipped the flag as we passed Beinn na Caillich and Corrie and the graveyard where my parents lie, and I tried to imagine death at sea. It seemed to me, that if one made friends with the elements, they would not be half so threatening.

'Come on, roll up!' I shouted to the vast lumps of swelling sea. 'We enjoy to climb you, no matter how high you get.' The crockery shattered and clattered below. My toothpaste fell in the cluggie . . . I was mortified about the boiled mutton, caper sauce and Skye potatoes I had prepared for lunch. We were all too miserable to touch it – that is, if we could even catch it before it all landed on the floorboards.

We got to Mallaig that night as a deplorably tired

crew, and no sooner had we clambered into our bunks than the most almighty blast went off (The Maroons). Someone was in trouble. The lifeboat was being summoned out – before you could say 'Jack Robinson' Ralph shot out of his bunk. His boyhood ambition was about to be realised. Joining the men congregating at the slip he volunteered to crew with them. His luck was in, they were one man short. I tossed and turned all night worried stiff about him. No one could have had a worse passage than we had already had that day; then to go and do it all over again in a raging storm (he needed his head seeing to). Our rubber fend-offs belched against the quayside, and at daybreak we found the saloon flooded. We had sprung a leak, surely? There was still no sign of the lifeboat, either. Everything had gone to hell.

Throwing on our yellow slickers John and I moved the boat round to a part of the quay where the tide would leave her high and dry. If we took out half her ballast and heeled her over, we could repair the damage done to her hull.

The lifeboat had got back about eleven. The missing boat with a minister and two boys on board had been found on the Isle of Pabay and there was no harm done. So, after a few drams with the lifeboat men Ralph thought about getting back to work again, and I noticed there was something wrong with his leg. The strain of humphing the tons of ballast was killing him. When we got it all stowed back in the bilges and the repair to the hull had been completed, we felt we were shipshape enough to sail home next day. Through the night, however, Ralph's leg got considerably worse. I tried to find a doctor. There was only one that I could contact, and he rather the 'worse for the weather'. But, after some strong coffee, he managed to diagnose a septic inflammation due to exposure and strain: 'The patient must lie up and then get hospital treatment.'

Now you would think that was bad enough. But no . . . there was more to come! When we looked for John the following morning to cast off and sail, there was no sign of him. No one had noticed him getting up and going ashore. We searched everywhere, and finally learned he had caught the south-going train to Glasgow – or London, for all we know – no explanations. He had actually jumped ship. We can only guess that it was an affair of the heart. He had made many telephone calls from Uig, and at his age perhaps they were urgent? But for us it was a major calamity. Perhaps we should leave the boat at Mallaig? But that would be letting the skipper down too. So Bert and I took separate watches, as we ploughed the heavy seas past Ardnamurchan Point again, with Ralph lying on his bunk in agony. I would have to get him to a doctor again as soon as we reached Oban. Bert would have to get hired crew there. But, as it happened, our luck was in. He found friends in Oban willing to escort him to Crinan, and there he met a well-known singing priest, who, with his boat-minded nephew crewed the rest of the way for him.

When we got home the doctor kept Ralph in bed for a fortnight, suggesting he needed a holiday. And as for me, I swore, 'Never again. It would be Spain next year – by air!'

But now that the fitting out season has commenced, and the sun is shining again, wild horses (or white horses) won't stop me. It's

Ultima Thule

Speed bonnie boat
Like a bird on the wing
Over the sea to Skye

once again.

Sadly, this idyllic lifestyle must come to an end. Kazik had been promoted. He had done some designs for the Hoover company. After inventing the pump system for the keymatic washing machine they wanted him to go to London and join their factory at Periwell. Hoover was offering a good deal more money and we just had to consider it. So we spent a week or two packing things up, storing things in the flat, arranging for my sister June to take my mother's flat over. Her husband had recently died and my brother Christopher had managed to buy a croft in Uig in Skye for her; we helped her arrange to take some of our furniture and all her possessions up to Skye.

We did this before leaving for London. We left the boat in the charge of the two lock keepers and hoped for the best. This turned out to be a mistake I had to deal with later. Finding ourselves a new home in or around London proved to be huge fun. All expenses paid in various luxury hotels until at last we found what we wanted. It was rather cruel of me, but I decided on Richmond, Surrey. After all I knew it well, having been stationed there as a Wren on boats during the War.

We found a charming but very expensive flat on Sheen Road. It wasn't far from Kew Gardens and very near to Richmond Park. But, oh dear me, it was so expensive living there I needed to have a job. I worked part-time selling gowns in Richard Shops and went to a wood mill, arranged to have some planks cut up into small squares. I got them home, started making icons. Kazik had told me that it was possible to make shallow carvings of the Virgin, put little halos and

crowns on her made from the lids of coffee tins. This I did and
sold them quite well around the antique shops in Richmond.
This helped a little, but we were anxious and worried finan-
cially.

So we discovered Our Lady Queen of Peace, the Catholic
church, as Kazik was Catholic of course, and got very friendly
with the priest whose name was Brian Maxwell. We had
delightful evenings drinking coffee with our feet up round
the fire discussing all kinds of subjects under the sun. It was
wonderful to have me, an ignoramus, sitting between two
brainy chaps, my own husband and this brilliant priest. In a
slow, unnoticeable way, the meaning of Catholicism became
clear to me. And I was invited to participate in the mass at
Easter.

My imagination was running riot these days, the mid-
1960s. I was so sad that I had no children I took to writing
poetry. I'd sit on a bench down by the river and write and
write. Then when I got home I would try to plonk out stories
for radio on a grotty old typewriter. And my poetry:

> Dead flowers and dynamite remind me of war,
> The flowers of corpses
> Strewn like children's toys
> Upon a nursery floor.
> What ferocious passion burns in man
> That all disasters he has known before
> Fade through love's sunshine
> To another day of strife and bloody gore.
> Yet nature still ignores
> And sets the scene for more.

The wind blows and stirs the memory of things gone
past. Had it been a purgatory or a gift? 'A privilege, some

might say! Childhood, hate, love and death – the pattern's the same – only the people are different . . . some crippled and maimed . . . some beautiful to look upon, with hearts of stone.

The trees quiver and shake as the wind intensifies. The old woman crouches nearer the fire. 'The coal should last till the next boat-load!' she calculates.

'Boat-load?' you ask.

Of course! Everything is delivered by boat to the Island. Islands are like that. Things are brought, stowed on them. That which departs goes of its own free will – the young, the birds – but never the old! They stay put, crippled with arthritis, knuckles gnarled and twisted like the roots of a tree upturned by lightning.

The old woman moved her lean MacKinnon hands on her lap, in an effort to straighten them. They had been beautiful once. She had even earned money with them – not by hard work but by having them photographed for advertisement . . . frail and delicate inside silk stockings, or holding a cigarette, their shape silhouetted through the smoke. Those were the days when money was tight and films were few and far between. The old woman chuckled . . . there was the time she had gone through the agent's window to avoid the fast-growing queue at the door. She'd got the part, too, a lady-in-waiting in a court scene with Conrad Voight as the Wandering Jew. They tried to burn him with real flames, men with fire-extinguishers trying to get near the scaffold on which he hung. (No wonder the Old Shepherd's Bush Studios went up in flames!) You got a cup of coffee free and a pound a day for shouting 'Banana! Banana!' in the crowd scenes.

'I believe they've changed it to "rhubarb" now,' she mused.

Yes! She must have been in six or seven films before the War. Where was that place outside London where a young man, about to become world-famous on film and stage had taken her to buy a bulldozer (of all things!) and her first high-heeled shoes had stuck in the mud; he'd carried her down a dark sinister alley when they had got back to town, claiming that he alone knew where you could find a cobbler on a Sunday. She'd felt like Oliver Twist being inveigled into the clutches of Fagin, for the old man that answered a rhythmic knock at the door had a beard that was nearly tripping him.

'Vot you vont? How much you got?'

And the leading star who never ever needed money (his name was enough) got her heel repaired with *her money*, her last half-crown!

The tears of rain on the windowpane moved slowly, down, down and sleep confused the continuity. She woke again with a start . . . the sirens! The nurses' white aprons fluttering before her eyes: American ambulances spewing out their wounded, laying them out on the ward floors to queue for beds and scooping the mud and debris from their eye-sockets, then noting the contents of their civilian pockets. Paraldehyde to keep them from climbing up the walls . . . Jesus himself on the operating table having the third amputation to the one leg. The old woman shuddered and blushed with shame . . . the escape . . . the train north . . . the Island again and the sea . . . the sea, the call of the sea! Then back into action once more at Plymouth port and the FS *Paris* riding the surf as a Wren.

'Stormy weather'. When would he come back? The channel was so wide . . . how long does it take to bleed to death? 'When he went away . . . stormy weather . . . you and I together.' The old woman's voice croaked to a halt and the tears transferred from the window to hang on the bones of her cheeks.

Her cheeks had not always been hollow. He (the loved one) had liked her lean face. 'Shows breed,' he said. 'Breed is important. The peasants' faces in Poland are wide – the cheeks like apples – Byzantine, perhaps? I marry you for the feet, the hands, the hair – all are long and elegant – so British. No? Cohania.' Yes! Cohania, yes! Yes! And she stretched her aged hands once more and knew that he had grasped them.

'The sky is overcast today,' said the man in the wellington boots.

'Yes,' said the other, 'it's like a Sunday . . . even the dogs don't bark . . . are you going to the funeral?'

'Me? No! I didn't know her that well. She kept herself to herself too much – no kind of a life that, sitting there letting the day follow the night in all its emptiness!'

I was making myself rather ill and very depressed, and one day scrounging round an antique shop on the Hill I discovered two black angels carved in wood. They were quite beautiful, long and narrow with very pointed wings. Like a fool I bought them. They would do for a birthday present for Kazik; I knew he loved woodcarvings.

No sooner had I brought them back home than things began to go badly wrong. My bright yellow Venetian blinds snapped shut and the sun went down on my horizon. We got a letter from the landlord saying that we would have to quit, giving us a month's notice. We'd never been very regular with our rent, and over and above that he said that the whole building was going under reconstruction. So there was nothing for it but to find somewhere else to live. Eventually we got a basement flat, a little house with a garden, the funniest place you ever saw in your life. It was a house within a house; during the War someone living there had built an air raid shelter inside the main living room.

It had a window and a door and was the cutest sort of little Wendy house you ever saw! I painted bricks all round the outside and put curtains on its little window, made a little bedroom inside it. There was not much to look at and you couldn't have furniture in it, except a bed, so I painted stars on the ceiling and funny-shaped clouds; Kazik and I would sleep in there. But with all the hard work and tension I found myself in the Richmond Hospital with a mild heart attack. This wasn't funny as Kazik would have to look after himself, which he was bad at doing.

Round about that time, in 1967 and 1968, there was an epidemic of flu all over London, and almost everybody got this frightful bug. Kazik went down with it, was in bed for three days and then got a kind of lockjaw and was terribly ill.

Telling it as it was in 1968, eight miles out of London as the crow flies, she ran wild-eyed, with wild flowing hair through the streets of Richmond, frantically looking for a brass plate that would indicate the existence of a doctor. Why had she not known? Why had she not guessed? She knew there was an epidemic of flu in London, that lots of people had died of it and were ill of it, but it never occurred to her for one moment that her big, strong, handsome Polish husband could catch a thing like flu after being all through the War, in the Resistance and everything. But there it was – he was very ill, he was dying – and she couldn't get a doctor! In the end she did manage to find a little lady doctor who said he would be fine, that he would be able to get up and go to work on Monday morning. This was Sunday night. We had been to mass and I thought it very odd that Kazik stood dead still in the middle of the road, turned me round and said emphatically, 'Ronishau, I love you, I love you!'

And of course I had said, 'Well, don't be daft, darling, hurry up!'

We lived on the fringes of Richmond Park at the time and early in the mornings I would collect my darling little Yorkshire Terrier and off we would go, striding through the park in the long grass and the bracken. I would of course take my shoes off, bare-footed I would pretend I was back in my native Isle of Skye, because I was often homesick. Sometimes I would be very much afraid because the keeper had told me that as many as twelve dogs in a day would be killed by the stags that came out of the forest and stampeded them. So one had to be very careful. And sometimes you would meet an early bird singing or an opera singer airing their lungs in a high-pitched voice, not thinking that they were being heard by anybody living. Sometimes there would be a dancer having a twirl, enjoying his or herself as you can in such a place with a breeze from the river and the sound of the birds in the trees. And the whole atmosphere, although it was so near London was quite, quite delightful. A school of ballet dancing wasn't far away, and sometimes, if you were lucky, peeping through the trees you might see Princess Alexandra taking a little stroll, followed by a mounted bodyguard. But that was not very often.

We lived on the edge of the park, what Kazik in his delightful accent called the 'perry-ferry', meaning the periphery, or what I call *ultima Thule*. Because for me it was the edge of the world, the edge of my life here and very soon I had to get away from it, I must get away to my own native island, the Isle of Skye, where I have always felt I belong. Meanwhile we lived in a ground floor flat with a basement, very odd with a very eccentric owner. He was a scientist and antique dealer. Inside our flat, someone had built an air-raid shelter and I had drawn brickwork on the outside and clouds all over the ceiling. In there the doctor came again and again until Kazik gradually ceased to breathe.

'Bronchial emphysema' they said, and before I could get a priest he had passed away.

So there was poor Kazik dead from three days' flu. Naturally, I was completely hysterical, so much so that my heart began to give out again and I had to have injections. The doctor had to stay with me all night and well into the next day. About a week later I was well enough to take the two black angels, try to return them to the antique shop. The proprietor took one look at them and said, 'Oh no, no. Oh no, I'm not taking them back!'

'Well,' I said, 'you can have them back for nothing. I don't want any money for them. I just don't want them.'

And he said, 'Neither do I. They haven't brought anybody any luck. I heard your husband died.'

I said, 'Yes.'

And he said, 'And his name was Rauszer.'

I said, 'Yes.'

And he said, 'Well, the man I bought them off's name was Rauszer – he owns the Richmond Hotel. When did your husband die?' And I told him and he said, 'Well, Mr Rauszer of the hotel died at exactly the same time.'

'Oh my God, so there must be some sort of evil connected

with them.' He agreed, said there was no way he would touch them. So I took them back to the house intending to burn them.

But when I came to figure out how I could burn them and if they would fit in the fireplace and all that, I got to my knees and started to pray. I asked myself and I asked God why I should be defeated by this evil. Why couldn't I conquer this evil? Why couldn't I live with this, and in any case what would it matter if it affected me any more, because really I had nothing further to live for now that Kazik was gone. So I got up and put them in a box, made them ready for packing away permanently, but I decided that I would not burn them.

The Wee Man

Brian Maxwell, the priest, attended to both Kazik's funerals. I say both, because there were two services. They put on a Requiem Mass in Our Lady Queen of Peace especially for him; made the church look marvellous, great long candlesticks with candles burning at the end of every pew, a most beautiful and soulful service. We went on then to the crematorium, because Kazik had stated that he wanted to be cremated.

This was quite a different cup of tea, or shall we say, kettle of fish. Cold and spiritless, there was no soul – it was grim. I was glad to get away from there. How very different to the Requiem Mass in our church. I'll quote the well-known verse:

> Jerusalem, Athens and Rome
> I would see them before I die,
> But I'd rather not see any one of the three
> Than be exiled forever from Skye

It was quite wonderful the way our priest Father Brian looked after me. He even brought a whole troop of boy scouts to the house to sort out my belongings, to take heavy bits of furniture and things I couldn't carry. He had them taken to the auction rooms. Some of my stuff I gave to the church itself and everything was beautifully packed and arranged, ready for Pickfords to transport it all to Skye. Before departing I got hold of one of the boy scouts and said, 'Look, could you take me to where they sell motor bikes?'

'Sure thing.'

So we went, and found a shop, and the scout helped me select a motor bike – I knew nothing at all about them and had never ridden one in my life. But it was a memento of England and I thought it would be handy in Skye. This would be an opportunity to get it put in the Pickfords van with all my stuff.

A lady of easy virtue who lived in the top floor flat of our building was also extremely helpful. Most of her clientele came from Heathrow, young airmen and the like. But she did have a good knowledge of the district and knew of a blitzed-out demolished house that had some gorgeous wrought iron railings smashed up and left lying about the garden. They were lovely things, probably Georgian, with a design of grapevines trailing right round. I saw the foreman, bought six and got the Boy Scouts to put them in the Pickfords van. And off they went. It was an enormous van and would only get as far as Fort William before it would have to unpack, put the contents into two smaller lorries, in order to go on the ferry for Skye. Otherwise, the boat would sink with the stuff I'd brought home with me! And this was the last of my money till Kazik's pension scheme had materialised. Then, I thought, I would be comparatively well off and able to buy my dream cottage in Skye. It was my firm intention to get there as soon as possible. With the help of my sister June I would find a little croft house, preferably with a barn attached, in which I could make a craft shop. After waving the van away and giving up my flat, I booked a sleeper from Euston Station to return North – after all Skye would always be my home.

My wonderful Irish priest saw me off at Euston Station, together with poor Kazik's ashes stowed in a sealskin bag my mother had once given me. So it was discreet, and I hoped the box would be comfortable in that container. The priest also gave me two beautiful, green Irish bath towels as a going away present, and I use them to this day. It was sad really, leaving London, but I was going to a far better place.

The journey as far as Inverness was comfortable enough in the sleeper. But when I rolled out in the early hours of the morning and crossed the platform, clambered into the waiting Kyle of Lochalsh train en route for Skye . . . things became shady, and weird, and unreal. It was an old train with single carriages . . . and I got one to myself. I placed the ornamental box covered with the little sealskin bag carefully on the seat opposite. Then the whole carriage seemed to go dark. Perhaps it was my eyesight, a blood clot behind my eyes or something, but the weird shape of a lady seemed to come into the carriage, sit down right beside the casket. She was dressed in black, she raised her veil, and to my astonishment I recognised her as Kazik's mother from a photograph I'd seen of that beautiful lady in Poland. She was gently smiling, in full sympathy with everything I was thinking; she accompanied me all the way to Kyle of Lochalsh. I wept and wept, and was not afraid, but then gradually she seemed to dissolve into the mist, the carriage lightened up again and everything was more or less normal.

It was flogging with rain when the train stopped, but I struggled down to the ferry. The furniture had not yet arrived, and wouldn't for a couple of days, so I was met by my cousin Angus Graham, who conveyed me all the way up to Uig, to stay with my younger sister June until I could find some place of my own. June gave me a warm and wonderful welcome with hot soup, a warm bed and everything one could desire. Then came the burial, this took place in Broadford.

There was a service for Kazik's remains to be put in a grave, one which I had already reserved for myself. I arranged for a local builder and his brother to build a long narrow cairn; I had a collection of semi-precious stones belonging to Kazik inserted into the cement, then I got them to top that with the Free French Cross. Kazik had spent so much time in the Resistance movement during the War and I thought that appropriate. It was in a beautiful setting overlooking the islands Scalpay and Raasay, one couldn't wish for a more beautiful spot to lie in.

Now I felt I must get on with my own life. I looked at many forlorn croft houses in the north end of Skye because I wasn't going to be able to spend much; I'd have the rest of my life to take care of so I couldn't afford much in the way of a house.

I saw one derelict place which was in an ideal position, up on the top of a hill surrounded by trees. Inside I noticed a couple of horns sticking out from the upstairs window; a cow had got there before me, had gone up the rickety staircase and got its horns jammed in the window. So I released and shooed it out, went on hunting for somewhere suitable. There was one house up the Conon River. It was a larger house, very quaint, but the thing about it, there was a rumour . . . they said it was haunted. Well, I had enough problems of my own in that direction. I was already hallucinating quite a lot: that business of seeing Cecilia, Kazik's mother, in the train, for instance. I was, after all, very disturbed, and took to writing poetry and wandering about in the hills all by myself, until eventually my sister contacted a solicitor called Cameron. He was an odd bod if ever there was one, but he was very intelligent and rather crafty; he sold me a croft house on the opposite side of the bay from my sister in Idrigill in Uig. We could always see each other, for she had a telescope and I had Kazik's opera glasses, so we could tell what each other was doing most days.

It was a two-acre croft house with a split gable end. But the leaking roof, faulty electricity and other repairs would cost me a great deal of money. The great thing about the house was the view: looking across the bay you could see the distant peaks of the Cuillin Hills. In the bay itself you could see the Klondykers, great fishing vessels that had come from Denmark and Norway, many of them, much to the delight of the local lassies, who found the foreign sailors on board these ships very intriguing.

I managed to get my gable end, the roof and all other repairs done by a local man. But what to do with the barn? It was huge, bigger and more useful than the house itself, with a workshop attached, just what I'd dreamed of. I managed to get a man from the village to come and help me, clear it, gut it, cement the floor, put steps up to it, clean off the woodwork. The cattle stalls were still in it, beautiful mature wood all greasy and shiny from the cows' necks rubbing against them, and we stripped, varnished and polished them. It was going to make a very good little craft shop; I hadn't a clue in the world how to begin and I certainly had no stock.

So, with the help of my sister I borrowed some household paint; I had brought no paints or brushes up from London. I had to fall back, if I was going to paint some landscapes, on using lipstick, make-up, sun-tan lotion, mixtures with linseed oil; I managed to create my own paints. I also got some hardboard cut, sized it and started painting. I had no knowledge as to whether they were any good or not, and I had nobody who could really tell me. So, gradually, I put some wheelbarrows in the little shop and decorated it all round with jerseys from the Outer Isles; I got a lady who could sew to make ponchos, as they were fashionable at the time. Even so I was very short of stock, and also short of customers. Till one day.

A wee bandy-legged man, if he was a man, came wandering up the croft through the sweet-smelling grasses, and past the beds of wild primroses. The smell in the air was intoxicating, far stronger than any alcoholic drink. He approached my little shop, now called Boskie's Barn after a story which Kazik had told me about a soldier called Boskie – everything he wished for seemed to come true. I hoped it would have that effect on me and in some ways it did!

For this little man was most weird . . . dressed as no one had seen anyone dressed before in the Isle of Skye. He was in very short shorts, clavery boots and to top it all he had a Tyrolean hat with a great feather stuck in the side. He wore a short-sleeved shirt and a leather waistcoat, all embroidered with intriguing designs and hammered-in copper tacks, buttons and beads. His accent was strange, too; it didn't seem to be foreign, just an out-of-the-world accent. He came to my shop, looked around and said, 'You're a bit low in stock, aren't you, dear?'

I said, 'Well, I've just started, you know. I'm painting these pictures and hope they'll sell.'

He said, 'Well, they should, they look good to me! But if you like, I'll give you a tip that'll bring you in any money you want. The more you work at what I tell you, the richer you'll become. But perhaps at the end of the day you won't want it.'

And I said, 'Oh, goodie goodie, tell me, what do you mean? What is this tip?'

And he started to explain: 'Get some dinner plates and a candle, and smoke the plates. Well, I can see for myself

you can draw, so draw some designs and some landscapes, whatever you fancy into the smoke, then fix them
and you'll find you'll make a fortune.'

'Well,' I said, 'that's all right, I could do all that, but
how, who can fix smoke?'

'Ah,' he said, 'that's when you make your fortune, when
you discover how – and that is up to you.' He assured me
that I would sell not only hundreds, but possibly thousands if I felt so inclined. I didn't believe him, of course.

But after he had gone I decided to try it out, his
methods of candling and etching into the plates. I had no
tools for the job so I used hairpins, anything I could find
really. I broke my neck experimenting with nail varnish,
ordinary varnish, ships' varnish and every kind of thing.
Of course, you couldn't put these plates in the kiln
because the smoke would disintegrate. But eventually
I did find a way of fixing them and it was quite true, they
sold hand over fist. I couldn't make enough of them. I
dried them off outside in the sun; intrigued customers
would buy six at a time.

So I got cracking and worked night and day. There
was no doubt about it, this was a miracle, like seeing
Kazik's mother in the train, seeing this little man from
outer space. Surely it must mean that Kazik or Someone
up there was giving me a badly needed helping hand.

> Dan, Dan, the lavatory man
> Underneath the ground all day;
> He combed his hair with a leg of a chair
> And it's anyone's guess what he might wear!

From the shore I collected driftwood and brought bits up to
my barn. At the side of the barn I'd had a local chap build a

working bench and put on a vice. I engaged him to do the heavier work screwing and sawing; I formed the bits of driftwood into all kinds of animals and people, which was great fun.

Then a television crew came to Uig doing a programme for the schools. They approached me – would I allow a bunch of children to go to the shore, help me gather driftwood and carry it up to my barn? Could they follow with the cameras? So I quickly agreed and it was fun, but it rained most of the time. I had to have them inside the barn, just full of silent children. They were all Highlanders from the north end of Skye, not rowdy. In fact, very shy, sweet and gentle; and the producer had a devil of a job trying to make them say anything at all, he didn't know what to do. He couldn't slap them!

So I got on the phone to the local shop to send up a crate of lollipops, ice-cream, and cakes, and we had a party. It was huge fun, you couldn't stop the children shouting and laughing. We made a very good film. I think they showed it two or three times.

Now that the rebuilding of my house was completed my furniture could come up from Dingwall, where it was on hold. It was an exciting and exhausting day. All the villagers gathered round offering to help. It was a nightmare trying to figure out how the amount of stuff I had could possibly fit into this little house. Most of it had to be put in the barn.

We laboured with the help of a young man called Murdo Buchanan, whom I was afterwards to employ in my workshop; and Angus the Loon, who was always ready to be helpful, provided you gave him a banana. Mad about bananas, they were his main diet. Money meant nothing to him, a dram was more important.

So we managed to get the stuff into the house; all the children and some of the men were very excited when they saw the motor bike coming out of this big van. They all wanted a hurl on it and ended up calling me 'Hilda Honda'; this name remained with me all the time I was in Uig.

One memorable character was Seadan the Post who was also a piper. He was a very useful go-between for my sister June on the other side of the bay and myself, although he was much more polite to me than he was to my sister. She lived at the bottom of a very steep hill and Seadan would be reluctant to clamber down and up again with her numerous parcels. She was addicted to what they called 'the book' – a catalogue system where you sent away for clothes, shoes and things for the children. Seadan would get rather fed up delivering these parcels; he would stand at the top of the hill, yell down at my sister in Gaelic, 'Oh, you lazy old besom, you can just come up and get this stuff yourself! I don't know what you want to be buying that rubbish for anyway!' And he would fit in a few swear words between every sentence. He didn't mean it, of course, and eventually her stuff would be delivered.

I only used the catalogue once myself. In 1971 there was a fashion for women to get wigs of all kinds. I thought it would be rather fun to send away for a silver grey one; that would suit me. About a week later it arrived in the Post Office. I was in busy looking at something (the Post Office sold everything from ham to shoes), when Seadan from behind the counter shouted out to a shop full of people, 'Hey, catch!'

I said, 'What?'

'Here it is, your wig's arrived.' I could have killed him!

The crofts in Idrigill were small, known as fishermen's crofts, the houses fairly close together. My next door neighbour was an elderly lady who was very religious, very strict, although she had a warm heart, could be very sweet and kind if it so came 'up her humph', as the saying goes. She used to do Bed and Breakfast. In the summer you would see her down at the gate waving her customers off, full of smiles, saying how she hoped they would come back soon again, what a pleasure it had been having them. Then, as soon as the car had departed, she would come up to my garden, push her way through the hedge, and red in the face start off in Gaelic deriding them. 'My droppings on them! Didn't they burn a hole in the sitting room carpet? Didn't he put his dentures in the bathroom in a glass and spill his detergent all over the floor? I hope I never see sight nor sign of them again!'

Well, that was Flora. She would sometimes ask me in for a cup of tea. She was awfully good at the pancakes but so religious, a typical Calvinist; afraid if anybody would see me, a Roman Catholic, in her house as she was Free Church or a seceder. One day I was sitting in her kitchen having tea and pancakes, enjoying a wee crack about everybody, everything and the weather, when who should turn up at her back gate but the Free Church minister! She grabbed hold of me by the arm, pulled me into the passage and said, 'For goodness sake, go into the dining room – you'll find the window is unlocked – climb through, and for heaven's sake don't let him see you in here or my days are finished!' I got home, sat down and roared with laughter. It was the funniest experience I think I'd ever had.

I had to practise with my Honda bike a little each day until I could get the hang of it. Going a little bit further, and a little bit further, I would reach Kensaleyre, go and visit Danny. Danny was an incredible character, used to be at one time butler and handyman at Skeabost. There are many tales that could be told about that period of his life.

At one time he went to sea, and when he was a sailor they went to Russia. He was introduced to the Czar of all the Russians, it was quite true. Actually, the Czar asked for him to be brought before him: he wanted to know what the Gaelic language sounded like and what Skye was like. And Danny had a long talk with him, brought back lots of souvenirs from his visit to Russia.

At that time he had a sister staying in their little croft house which was most unique – full of souvenirs from all over the world. Down by the loch was a deserted water-mill, a rather spooky place – the tools, sacks and lots of signs were left there. It is said that Danny's sister never moved away from the croft except once, and that was to go to Portree, not very far away. When she got there she was so horrified and terrified of the people, the build-ings, the traffic, the noise, that she got back home as soon as she could and never left her croft again for the rest of her life.

A few miles further down from Danny's house, nearer Portree, it is rumoured there is a lady who will give her favours to any gentleman, or any man for that matter, in exchange for a can of paraffin. Whether this is true or not I'm not certain.

There were a great many stories, true and untrue, told of an evening in my little house. Doctor MacRae would come round, my sister June and quite a few friends would exchange experiences. Some of them were sad, and some very funny.

Dr MacRae told of a nurse who was in the district at one time and she had to go to a very outlandish croft house to someone seriously ill. It was a dull, misty morning. She thought she would take a shortcut across a stretch of boggy peat land to reach the neighbouring cottage; she thought she would be safe enough in her wellington boots. What looked like a lochan or a puddle was, in fact, quite a deep bog this day, and she stepped on some moss and sank right down to her armpits.

She struggled to get herself free and trying to gain a footing she clambered on to a rock. She felt under her feet what she took to be a large rock, and, scrambling on, she was able to see above the water. But it sank under her weight and suddenly she felt herself being raised higher and higher . . . a huge hairy monster rose up in front of her, with a great pair of horns trailing weed and nostrils alive with maggots. A maggoty, revolting head of a dead bullock was under her feet! She nearly had a heart attack, yelled and screamed, and worst of all found that she was now covered in beasties herself!

Fortunately the whole village heard her screams and she was rescued and told she had been standing on the rump of a dead cow which had sunk in there ages ago; by mistaking its backside for a rock and standing on it the head had risen up.

As for the maggots, they are just maggots – alcohol is as good a disinfectant as any other – 'and who should know that better than yourself, being a nurse', was all the comfort anyone could offer her.

But there were many other times since Kazik's death that I would feel lonely and sad and very tearful. Sometimes I would go to the window at night and look across the Uig Bay at the Klondykers swinging on anchor with their lights all glittering. It was a beautiful sight and very soothing. One Saturday night I turned away to warm my hands at the fire and looked up above the mantelpiece, saw my wooden carving of Kazik's face. I'd been crying a lot and to my utmost astonishment I watched a large tear ooze out of the left eye, roll down the cheek and drop onto the mantelpiece. I put my finger out and felt it, because I couldn't believe what I saw; my finger was wet. What Kazik had prophesied all that long time ago when I was carving this object had come true.

Needless to say I had no sleep that night and got up very early. It was Sunday and my intention was to take out the motor bike and go all the way to Portree to mass. For most of the way the ride was very enjoyable; it was wonderful to see the changing colours in the sky, those streaks of duck green, purpley mauve and orange as the sun was rising. It was winter, very cold and I had no gloves. I was driving fast. When I got to Portree and came to the church like an idiot, I decided to show off my new Honda. So I took a turn round in front of the church and fell off my bike, head over heels, arse for elbow and a whole lot of the people going into the church came rushing over. I felt an absolute fool. There is no doubt about it, as the Bible says, pride comes before a fall.

However, the priest was concerned. He was an awfully nice man, so he got me into his car, delayed the service, and took me to the Portree Hotel where he obtained bandages, ointment and, to top it all, a large brandy. That was all very cosy, I felt a lot better, but very much ashamed of myself. I sat through the service and after it was over the priest and a friend of his took me home. This friend was an Irishman with a very earthy sense of humour. I made lunch for them with roast potatoes rubbed in olive oil and covered with garlic salt, put the sign of the cross on them, thinking that would be appropriate. There was a pot of stew, and so we all enjoyed a good lunch with a good glass of wine. As we were sitting in the sitting room there was a scraping at the back door, like an animal scratching. I went to investigate and lo and behold who should be there but my sister Morag all the way from New Zealand; she hadn't let us know she was coming or that she was in this country at all! It was a huge surprise and we laughed, hugged, cried, and were just delirious with happiness.

And when we calmed down I began to wonder how we could get a message to my sister June to come across and join us. The rather wicked Irishman suggested he would go and tell my sister, he'd take his car and bring her across. We agreed. But he then suggested I should lie down on the couch and be covered with a rug. He would tell my poor sister that I'd taken a bad turn; the priest was with him, and he wasn't very sure he wasn't going to give me the last rites. This was a wicked thing to do. However, June got into his car and they drove hell for leather to my house. June rushed over to the couch, pulled back the rug – and nearly fainted when she saw it wasn't me but Morag, in full health and in great form! It was a naughty joke to play but she survived it.

It is good to look back on those happy days in Idgrill and my two sisters. There would be fork lunches at Skeabost, open-air pageants organised by Dr MacRae and his pals in which my younger sister would take part. There would be sails to the Outer Isles to Lewis and Harris, cosy céilidhs at home, especially at New Year when the house would be full of people and Flora from next door would come with her one annual bottle of whisky and share it round with everybody. She would carry one glass and as each person took a dram she would clean the glass with her thumb, very thoroughly, before handing it on to the next. God bless her, she was a great comfort living near and being so kind!

I became very friendly with the tinkers, too. They used to mend brass jeelie-pans for me and collect the cas chrom – a peat digger, or primitive plough used in the old days with the foot, to dig out trenches before planting the potatoes. I did a lot of dealing with the tinkers. They would find things they knew I would want to sell in my little shop. And I would buy dozens of baskets from them, beautifully hand-made, to hang on the rafters in my shop, the house and workshop.

The ones in the workshop were full of Murdo – the young man who used to help me – full of his tools, nails, screws, glues, things needed in a workshop. It was very good to stow them hanging in these baskets. I used to tease and remind him they were full of lost boys as in *Peter Pan*.

Murdo was a bit of a Peter Pan himself. He was a quiet, gentle and very loveable person. Sadly, one weekend he and his wife and friends went over to the Outer Isles to Lewis; they were walking along the road after a concert, perfectly sober, when a car came towards them and Murdo moved himself and his family into the ditch to let it past. Then, foolishly, without turning round he walked back into the centre of the road; there was a car coming behind him and it knocked him to kingdom come. He was in fact decapitated. The funeral they had for him was the biggest I ever saw in the Isle of Skye. It was very, very sad and my heart went out of the shop really altogether. Everything seemed to go wrong after that.

For one thing, the currency was changed. Now, I had never been to school except to Drumfearn when I was very little, as I'd always had a delicate heart. And apart from sharing governesses with my cousins in Skeabost, I really had no education. So to cope with the new money, to keep my books in order and think like that became far too much for me. One sunny spring morning a minister came. He was back from Vietnam and he stood on the steps I'd made in front of my little barn.

It was a glorious sunny morning; he raised his head and breathed deeply, said, 'Oh, what I would give to have a little place like this!'

Impulsively, I put my hand out and said, 'Right, mate, what would you give?'

And I sold the whole place on the spot. I really regretted it afterwards because the property prices in Skye had soared. When I came to find somewhere else to live, it was a different story. My cousin Angus from Kyleakin offered to take me round in his car looking for somewhere within my means. We could find nothing suitable. So he suggested I take a look at his shepherd's cottage down by the sea at Lusa.

'It was falling to bits,' he said, 'but maybe you could do something with it.'

So we went down and took a look at Lusa Farm Cottage. The position was quite out of this world; it was facing the Island of Pabay and had Raasay and Scalpay, a panoramic view all round. I really fell in love with it. But it would take every penny I had in the world to put it in order. I would have to start digging the foundations. It would need re-roofing, water, electricity, a septic tank, you name it; everything.

However, I went to see the banker at Kyle of Lochalsh and he seemed unusually friendly. When I said who I was, he knew all about me. He said, 'Did you share a flat with my aunt in London, Anne MacKintosh, the nurse who was born in Breakish?'

'Yes, most happily I did for some considerable time,' I replied.

He said, 'She's told me so much about you. I'd be happy to advance you a loan.'

So I went ahead. Angus and I went to see the solicitor in Portree and he made out an agreement between us that 'I would have the house at Lusa and some of the ground for one shilling until the day I would die, and thereafter I would quit with all my belongings.' A rather funny wording, I thought.

We were extremely happy about it and I managed to contact some workmen who came from Leith. They said they were going to be on strike for some considerable time, during which they would undertake to rebuild my house. So I chanced it. Well, they made a pretty good job of it, were thorough, got the water and electricity in, a bathroom, and it really was charming. But they never got round to finishing a front porch that was in the contract, a suntrap at the back of the house and the staircase; so you had to go up to the first floor on a ladder. I used to climb it and go to bed with a long iron poker at my bedside in case there would be intruders. You see, the Leith men's strike was over and they simply moonlighted. However, I did manage to get a workman through from Portree and another wee Irishman. They agreed at a reasonable cost to build the two porches and staircase. I was very sorry to lose the original spiral.

Follow the Seagulls

Angus Graham's farmland at Lusa stretched from Kyle House down to the Lusa River on both sides of the road. It used not so very long ago to stretch right across to Kylerhea, over the top of the mountain. At shearing time there would be a couple of shepherds climbing up Beinn na Caillich Kyle, as we called it, from Rudha na Caillich and Kylerhea; Angus and some of his men would climb up from the Kyleakin side and meet at the top. They would drive all the sheep down to the fank near Aiseag on the other side of the river. The fank was a magical place.

When we were young we used to take a little maid called Fanny Gunn who played the melodeon, Angus Graham on the pipes, my brothers and sisters and myself, all the Grahams and all the MacLeods, go to the fank at midnight, have great feasts there, swim in the moonlight, dance and have a hilarious time. But that's not what I'm on about. Lusa, unfortunately, allowed an airstrip to be put as close as you could imagine – almost right on the top of the Pulpit Rock.

Now the Pulpit Rock is very sacred, near the graveyard at Aiseag. There's a rock which is formed rather like a chapel, the river runs in front of it. On the other side of the river not far from there is a holy well. It really is holy. There was also at one time a very large tree, a bell used to hang on it; when Saint Maolrubha came over from Ireland, and possibly Saint Ninian as well, they would preach at the Pulpit Rock. They would ring the bell on the tree, people would come to be converted to Christianity. Before that they could have been anything, moon worshippers mainly, fully pagan. It is said that as many as five hundred people were converted in the one day. But right up till now, people are beginning to discover the holy well. I don't think they have yet discovered much about the Pulpit Rock. My father was very knowledgeable about it.

In those far off days in Breakish when I was a young girl and my two brothers were even younger, my father would try to avoid spending Sundays cooped up in the old Breakish house where no one was allowed to read, do work or do anything creative. So, my father used to get hold of an empty whisky bottle and fill it with milk, make some sandwiches, take myself and my two brothers, and we would sneak off down to Aiseag. He would give us a wee sermon at the Pulpit Rock then send us off to collect some very large shells, as large as we could find, and we would bring them back to the Rock; he would use them as cups, pour milk into them. Then he would give us each a piece of scone or some cheese, whatever he had managed to scrounge from the house.

My father was a Chauvian character – very much so – he believed in keeping the body fit and his wayward mind could take care of itself.

Apart from his daily dip in the ice-cold Atlantic waters he would afterwards wander off with a couple of old golf clubs down to the so-called golf course at Aiseag, where the grassland by the sea was cropped short by munching cows. If he knew I was jogging along behind him – a would-be caddy – he would smuggle a couple of treacle scones and a bottle of milk into his enormous poacher's pockets, and I would race to the edge of the sea to find a couple of large shells to drink it from. We would sit in the shade of the great Pulpit Rock, where the monks had gathered to listen to the words of St Maolrubha away back in Columba's times.

As we sat there watching the setting sun we would make up verses:

> The flicker of a candle
> The flutter of a butterfly's wings
> The shadow on a wall
> Marginal things all.
> Dawn of day and fall of night
> The power behind a Heron's flight
> No shaking hand or tired mind
> Can ever really try to find . . .
> The answer.

My father often made poetry:

> I contemplate the little world
> Where ferns are trees
> And bits of grass are fences
> Where dragonflies are aeroplanes
> To bomb the ant's defences.
> I kneel among the clover buds
> With Lilliputian care,
> I'll never be too old or wise
> To make a little prayer –
> For Grasshoppers, and Mice and Me
> God is everywhere.

But somehow or other he never looked quite right in this rugged and romantic place after all these years of living in the Isle of Skye. My father had never really become a Sgitheanaich. Like an old man who might have cradled in the arms of a luscious young mistress he always looked funny and out of place. They nicknamed him 'The Pope'. To my mind his setting was always art nouveau: a shining piano set in the window draped with Spanish shawls, a photograph of my mother set in an ornate little frame, a blue jar of orange cape gooseberries in the window ledge.

Of course my mother could never stand for the like of that much. When she would have my father returning home from the hill, strolling through the garden calling softly 'Coo-ee, coo-ee – Mary – are you there?'

Of course she was there, wasn't she always there, where else would she be?

So off we'd go the next day up the hill and past the fank, where the dipping was in full swing, the shearing of a great number of sheep always excited me. And as we proceeded higher and higher into the mountain the squelching multicoloured peat moss soaking my bare feet I would start to sing accompanied by the gurgling music of the river.

'Do you hear it, Father?' What is it saying? Stop a minute and listen . . .'

My father would grin and nod his head – 'That's right, my girl,' he'd say.

'Can't make out a word of it myself, it sounds like Gaelic. Maybe you'd know.'

Then we would settle again with our scones and milk, and pretend to build a house of loose bits of rock, encrusted with grey lichen. He was the architect, three bedrooms, kitchen, dining room, drawing room. I always had to remind him to build the bathroom – he was never very practical – and I did the furnishings from peat moss, leaves and fern. And the people we entertained were fairies.

Now perhaps you don't believe in fairies, but we did, and we proved it. Because some of the music he played on the old piano, when we got back home at night was the same as we heard by the river that day – at any length so I thought.

After the session on Sundays at the Pulpit Rock we would have to give a thanksgiving offering to the holy well. We didn't have any pocket money, so he suggested we give the well a flower and make a wish. And this we used to do.

I was very keen on it because I felt strongly that all my wishes would one day come true. I would go and gather daisies, buttercups or whatever happened to be growing at the time, apart from the watercress that is always there. I would kneel down on the slab of rock that was placed in front of the holy well and say my prayers. There were little ledges either side, and I would put in a daisy, a little pretty pebble or shell and fervently wish for whatever it was in my mind . . . I think I did more wishing than praying.

Well, back to Lusa. I have a strong feeling that some of those monks who used to pray at the Pulpit Rock at Aiseag lived at Lusa because the marking of a very much larger house is there. Lusa Farm Cottage was never called a cottage in Gaelic, it was called Taigh Lusa, implying it was more of a house. When I started digging, trying to create some sort of garden, I came across little inkbottles, quite ancient, buttons (God knows when they were made) and the like. It is said, my grandmother told me, that monks lived on the Island of Pabay and at one time there was a subterranean passage coming all the way from the Island of Pabay to the Pulpit Rock. I'm sure the whole place is magical. There is every sign houses were around, too, as there are all sorts of ruins. One particular favourite of mine was the spirit of an old lady who I was convinced lived there one time.

Whenever I felt lonely or depressed, fed up, I would walk along to Aiseag and have a chat with her.

I would stand at the opening of the ruined building by the Rock and she would say in Gaelic, 'Gabh a stigh!' (come in) And I would. In my mind she was saying have a cup of tea, do this, do that, 'Dean suidhe' (sit down) and so on and weirdly I would find myself doing everything she told me. She was a friendly old girl and I think her name had been Seonaid.

Funnily enough, there was quite a deep well just at the side of this ruined old house. My grandmother used to tell me so much about wells. At the house where I lived in Idrigill was a well with a little iron pipe coming out of it where the water flowed down from the River Rha; frequently a little trout would come swimming down. My grandmother told me of a well on the Island of Rona resurrected by Professor Darling about forty years ago. In it he maintained he could see the Virgin Mary. Whether he was trying to create a British Lourdes or not, I don't know, but that's what I was told when I used to stay at Skeabost. Professor Darling used to come and stay with my Uncle Duncan. He made many visits to the Island of Rona and was deeply inspired by the holy well.

There were plenty of sinister ones, too, especially in the north end of the island. Sometimes in order to get rid of rats, if the well was near the house, they would cover it with tissue or soft paper, and put cheese or food on top; the rats would come in the night, jump onto the paper and fall into the well. If anybody was about there was a better chance of shooting them. Many a weird thing must have been dropped down those wells in the old days – even perhaps an unwanted baby – and one story I heard when I was young concerned a man who committed a murder.

A lot of white ox-eyed daisies grew round the well at his house, and he would go and drink there. Every time he went to drink at the well blood would splatter all over the white daisies. He got so frightened about this, realising that if that went on people would get suspicious, and accuse him of this murder.

So he packed up and, I believe, took the first ship to Canada and was never heard of again. Because they do say, if you cross over water you can rid yourself of an unpleasant ghost.

Personally, I find ghosts so pleasant and so chatty, so nice and comforting to be with that I wouldn't cross water to be rid of them at any time! My own resident ghost at Lusa was a young woman, plump, rosy-cheeked, black-haired; a very comfy, cosy sort of ghost. Her name was Katie.

Of an evening when I'd furnished my house and got it completed, I would sit at a colossal peat fire and chuck on branches of wood, settle down in a lovely, handmade, high-backed basket chair that I had bought when I lived in Idrigill. It had been made specially for a man who must have had dropsy he was so colossal. It was the hugest basket chair I'd ever seen, but I filled it with cushions, and, with a stool at my feet I would relax and listen to Katie telling me her little stories, which, I'm afraid to say were mostly connected with vomit. She ate a lot and I suppose died of what she ate.

So she was always telling stories about how this old man had come home drunk as a lord and had been sick all over the floor. He had many children (sixteen, I think it was). They were all so hungry and starving, they encouraged the old man to be sick.

And they would jump round him excitedly, shout out in Gaelic, 'Spew big bits, daddy. Spew big bits!' Oh, they had to get their protein somehow or other.

During the day in bad weather I would spend my time painting in oils. Dear cousin Angus had knocked together a great easel with very coarse wood, put a couple of huge nails either side and a plank across. I would perch a lump of hardboard or plywood up on the board, then go off into a sort of trance and paint like mad, non-stop, without food or cups of tea, paint and paint until I thought I'd got it pretty well finished. I never took more than two days over any painting (see plate 24).

On other days I would order from Glasgow hundreds of coarse china plates, mostly from shipping stores. I'd smoke them, etch into the smoke, do my secret fixing. Then I would beg MacGregor the butcher, or whoever came down with a van once or twice a week with food, fish or coal, to deliver my efforts to the various shops in Broadford, Kyleakin, Portree, all over the island. In this way I made my bread and butter.

On very fine days I would take a couple of buckets, some rubber gloves and off I'd go to the whelks. I rather enjoyed this, although grovelling about looking for these little creatures, I think, is very bad for the eyesight. My two dogs, Barnabus the collie and Kiwi the Yorkshire Terrier, would accompany me and stay with me the whole time. I would spend hours on the shore until I was very, very tired; when I got into that state I would frequently see the spirit of Katie ahead of me, her wide skirts floating out in the breeze, looking just like a ship with sails. She would come close, whisper in my ear, 'You would find more whelks if you went out onto the rocks stuck in the grooves of the rocks.' Or, 'Go a little to your left and you'll find masses of seaweed all knotted together looking quite like spaghetti; under these piles you would find more whelks, my dear.'

She was very companionable. Sometimes on a very low tide she would say, 'Walk further out. Go right out, as far as the wee island. Just follow the seagulls.' And sure enough I would paddle out to the wee island and find big whelks sitting on top of seaweed that looked for all the world like rhubarb leaves. The little island was called Eilean Fhearchair and was so tiny that if you laid down flat, your head would be touching one end of it and your feet the other. Katie's spirit was very much with me when I was out whelking. She would ask me loads of questions and then answer them herself – or was it me and my mind that was answering? – I don't know. She would say, 'You know, all these whelks are unisex,' and then have a good giggle. Then she'd say, 'You know that there is a hunk of cheese inside every thistle head.' And giggle again. 'And did you know that if you happen to be stung by a great big ink-fish, you would never ever have rheumatism for the rest of your life? And did you know that if you touch or sit on weasel's pee you would die? If you didn't die that way, the weasel would jump up and bite you in the throat – you would certainly die.' Oh, she was a caution right enough! And it is absolutely true.

One day I was having a swim. It was a gorgeous hot day and I'd brought with me an orange. I snuggled up against a warm dyke. The stones were comforting and I'd had a good long swim, my costume was drying in the sun. I was heating myself by the stones and I'd put my orange down in the long machair grass. Then I peeled it, didn't eat it all at once, put it back on the grass; a very big mistake. This was a dyke well known to have weasels in it. You could see them frolicking about, jumping from stone to stone, especially in the half-light of an evening. There were stoats as well, and sometimes an otter. The otter lived mainly in the coal-bunker. I'd often seen it. But, to get back to the weasel. Lo and behold!, after eating that orange, I became violently ill. And the next thing I knew I was in an ambulance being driven away to Inverness, put in an isolation ward with what they were calling salmonella poisoning. But of course I knew very well it was weasel's piss poisoning. It was very funny seeing all those doctors and nurses coming in covered with rubber gloves and great big gowns, masks on their faces, as though they were going to be contaminated any minute. I was there for about a week and was very ill, but survived to come back to my beloved Lusa.

Fit again, on the saner days, I would help Angus drive the sheep into the new fank, get them ready for shearing and dipping. I don't think I was much help but I did go back to the house, prepare sandwiches and tea, bring a basket to the men. There would be lots of jokes, bawdy, mostly in Gaelic, the men never thinking I could possibly understand. I enjoyed them just as much as they did. Sometimes the sheep would stray out at a low tide to Eilean Fhearchair and get stranded. When the tide came in, and sometimes they had their lambs, they would be afraid to swim ashore. So one day, feeling particularly noble, I decided to wade out on a low tide and drive the sheep off the island. I learned afterwards they are much better left to find their own way back. If a human being starts to drive them they panic, will frequently swim in the wrong direction and never be seen again. However, I was trying to encourage them to swim ashore when the tide came in rapidly. Now, there was no sand to be seen and it was a case of saving my own life, with a very long swim to the shore. More, I assessed, than I could possibly manage.

Luckily a nephew of mine had left a rowing boat and some oars behind when he came up on holiday. Angus saw my difficulty, came rushing down, got into the boat and started to row towards me. I'd started to swim towards him. Angus soon realised he couldn't get me into the boat without capsizing it. He didn't want to risk that because he couldn't swim himself, so he had the bright idea of flinging me a rope. Believe it or not I was towed ashore. It took me a long time to live that one down.

One day in early summer my cousin Angus kindly presented me with my very own peat bog. He and his brother Iain would come down each day and help me to dig the peats. I got quite expert at it, forming them into little pyramids to dry off, carting them home on an old perambulator that was falling to bits, but nonetheless was very useful. It was easier than carrying them in creels. My back would never be strong enough for that caper which my ancestors had always done. I felt very virtuous when I would be able to get my own peat stack built neatly against the gable end right up as high as the chimneys. It would give me lots of fuel for the oncoming winter.

Winters were hard, the January of 1981 exceptionally cold. Frozen trees were growing on the windows, the mountains like fairyland. Papa Joe, a fellow whelk gatherer in summertime called early in the New Year and I gave him his dram. He had been in bed for more than a week with the flu, but he was cheerful as ever with some funny stories to tell.

Papa Joe, when not at the whelks, helps his wife with paying guests, and for three years running now they have had a little man from China. He is very odd – insists on coming down to breakfast upside down! He keeps going in and out of the house like that (walking on his hands), saying it's good for his blood pressure. 'You could understand it if he came from New Zealand,' Papa Joe says.

One winter when Angus's brother Iain was having a coffee with me it was flogging with rain outside, simply teeming down. I had put too much wood and peat on the open fire and the chimney had gone up in flames. Now I'd always prided myself in coping with a chimney fire so I got my crock of salt and a bucket of cold water, lots of wet rags and gradually put the fire out. But my cousin Iain was agitating, 'Get the fire engine, get the fire brigade!' I got fed up, so I went to the telephone and rang them up; they said they'd be down immediately. Of course, by the time we saw them coming along the road bleep-bleeping their light, the fire was almost completely out, and the terrible thing was, with all the sodding rain the fire engine stuck in the mud. They couldn't get it to move! About twenty men were working away trying to pull this wretched machine out from thick mud – they even connected their hoses to the nearby seawater, to try and flush the wheels free. But it was no use. So they came down to the house and telephoned for another fire engine to come and pull the first one out. In due course it arrived, and also stuck in the mud.

Meanwhile, all these men, beautifully dressed in their dark blue uniforms with shining buttons and no overcoats whatsoever, no oilskins, no sou'westers – one or two of them had these yellow helmets – were absolutely soaked to the skin. And there was no way the second fire engine could pull the first one out! So in the end they had to go and commandeer a bulldozer some workmen had left at the side of the main road; they brought it down and eventually loosened both fire engines. But it was about eleven o'clock at night before they finally got them free. I gave them all a good dram and a good telling off – they ought to have realised it was dangerous to come down that road in such weather and they ought to have had oilskins to wear in such terrible conditions.

Some of the winters in Lusa were ferocious; high winds throwing the tide right up to the front door. Seaweed would be lying in front of the door when I opened it up in the morning. The great howling winds coming down the chimney made noises like banshees. Leaking roofs: I had to re-do and re-slate my Ballachulish slate roof at least three times. This was exhausting, re-building Lusa was no mean task. Feeling not at all well made me more irritable than usual. I'd get quite cross with the tourists, the geologists and the winkle-pickers who all came wandering down to the house.

The winkle-pickers especially, hanging their pails on my fence, and their jackets, crowding me out on the beach. One chap in particular, a retired policeman with loads of money, so I understand, used to come so close to me picking the whelks that I got very annoyed indeed. One day, accidentally on purpose, I pushed his bucket of whelks over and spilt the lot. He was dancing with rage.

'The Lord will punish you,' I shouted, 'you see if he doesn't!'

And with that the poor blighter swung round and slipped on the seaweed, falling flat on his face in a deep salt-water pool. His plastic oilskins swelled up like an inflated dinghy, his face scarlet and his language even more so; he looked for all the world like a hippopotamus having a dip. I ran for my life! Later I felt very ashamed about my lack of control; however, I never did see that man again.

I felt so guilty I thought it was time I restarted going to mass. This wouldn't be easy because I would have to hitchhike or walk to Kyleakin, then cross the ferry, where I would get the bus the church put on in those days. Each Roman Catholic paid a pound and got taken from Kyle of Lochalsh to Dornie to Saint Duthac's Church. I was so eager to get back to the fold in fact that I would take a lift from anyone. Sometimes it would be the Mother's Pride bread van and sometimes it would be a lorry, and on one occasion a car stopped. I was a bit frightened; I didn't care for the idea of going into a strange car, but this man seemed gentle and respectably dressed, so I risked it. I got in and became nervous. When I'm very nervous I talk too much: I prattled on about every subject under the sun. And sometimes I get very earthy, not too careful with my language, I try to be funny. What a great mistake! This man insisted on taking me as far as the church itself and dropping me at the door. I went into church, knelt down, said my prayers and the mass commenced. Lo and behold! who should be the priest but this man who'd given me the lift! If I can blush I certainly did that day. I was terribly embarrassed and tried to think what on earth I'd been talking about all those miles in the car with the man; he never told me he was the priest and was going to take the service that day. So, I don't think I ever took a lift in a car again.

One day when I'd turned up rather too early for mass in the Mother's Pride van I was very surprised to see Ted Murphy standing outside the church. He wasn't our regular priest, and I hadn't seen him for a good many years. So I said, 'Good lord, am I seeing a ghost?'

And he suddenly said, 'Rhona, Rhona, don't, don't say that, for God's sake! Don't say that!'

I said, 'Well, why not?'

And he said, 'Because I just arrived and went upstairs to talk to the priest and found him lying dead on the floor. How did you know there was a ghost here?'

I was very taken aback and didn't know what to say. This old priest had been very eccentric. He was determined to pass as a Highlander and wore the kilt regularly. He was so proud of his kilt that he used to pin his surplice up with a large safety pin so that people would be able to see his Highland hose and tartan kilt – just a peep of it anyway. The poor old man was a bit heavy on the bottle and wasn't very well for some time. He used to be very good at telling stories and knew his Scottish history inside out. It was he who told me that Loch Duich was called after St Duthac.

It was around this time that Lady MacDonald, a recent convert, joined the congregation. She was pregnant with the future Lord MacDonald of MacDonald of the Isles, and she struck me as a very gentle and kindly person; there was no side about her, no showing off or nonsense. She would sometimes read the lesson and would always offer me a lift back to Lusa, and I accepted. So we became good friends and after the birth of her son and heir, she invited me to his christening, a fabulous affair. The old Kilmuir Church was filled with flowers and the MacDonald family were all seated in their special allotted seats, coffined off with their own private pews. There was only one snag, the weather was absolutely atrocious: it was a ninety-mile-an-hour gale, wind and rain coming down in torrents.

The Day of the Christening, Sunday 2 May, 1982, it poured, snowed, thundered and just about everything short of a hurricane. No question of straw hats and silk dresses. I wore a light jumper under a silk-wool dress topped with my Sherlock Holmes cape, velvet hat and umbrella. Then after cooking a chicken and leaving electric fires on, to counteract the extreme cold, I waited till the lovely blonde Angela Fox came to collect me. We set off to arrive at the old Kilmuir Church, surrounded by its ancient trees, crypts and tombs. It was like walking into a Brontë or Dickens novel – the family within the church, the oil lamps, tall ornate stands to light the enclosed area reserved for MacDonalds, the immensely high pulpit as near Heaven as it can get; eerie stray leaves skirling and clutching round the tall, narrow windows, the trees outside fighting with the wind yet demanding to be let in.

At the foot of the pulpit was the young Lady Mac-Donald with the little Hugo MacDonald of Sleat in her arms, his long delicate christening gown, handed down for generations, draped nearly to the floor; so nice to see, because nowadays they usually put babies in little frocks.

The first reading was done by Lord Godfrey himself, and her Ladyship did the second reading. The hymns were cheerful and appropriate, the flower arrangements magnificent.

My heart went out to the kilted Breakish piper blowing his guts out, the rain blocking the drones and gusts of wind driving up his kilt. He must have been utterly miserable but he played on. The organ was played throughout by the younger brother Archibald MacDonald, and the reception held at the Ardvasar Hotel where the ladies were ushered up to room number eight to dry off. There were more than two hundred guests and plenty of champagne corks flying. We ate and drank merrily.

On reaching home, catching up with the news from the Falklands War was not easy after such a day, a day when it was totally swept aside. The newborn Hugo was the topic. It was his day. But the night was God's, the thunderstorm frightening. Alone again, with the dogs barking and needing comforting, we huddled together; it was very scary but we knew it would pass, like everything else.

Rebuilding Lusa had taken an awful lot out of me and there was still more to come, so to speak, in that I began to have awful pains. The doctor said I would have to have a hysterectomy. So they sent me over to Inverness, to Raigmore Hospital, for the operation and I afterwards had to go for a spell to my sister in Uig to recuperate. When I got home again I felt very restless. As I'd made quite a lot of money with my smoky plates, doing hundreds of them, painting in oils as well, I'd put enough aside to make me think I should have a holiday. So, impulsively, I went to the telephone and phoned my sister-in-law in Liverpool, asked her to book me a flight to New Zealand. I had quite a yen to visit my sister Morag, and didn't want her to know I was coming, she would only fuss. My sister-in-law went along with this and booked me a passage to New Zealand. So I travelled down to Liverpool and then on to Kent, where I stayed with my niece Catherine, Morag's daughter, for a week. She saw me onto the plane at Heathrow.

I remembered Kazik saying, 'If you find yourself going a long distance by air you should ask the steward to keep bringing you these small bottles of champagne, not the large ones but the little ones, keep them going and take sips of that until you reach your destination. You will find that you have no jetlag whatsoever.' So this I did. The steward brought along a little bottle. I sipped at it until we set off, and went via the Arctic Circle, because the pilot found he had to come down in Canada to change the crew who had caused a bit of trouble. So that gave me a chance to have a glimpse of Canada.

On we went to Los Angeles where I had a booking made to stay overnight in a hotel, but I cancelled that; one look at Los Angeles put the fear of death in me. I knew if I moved any distance at all I would be lost forever. So I went on standby for another plane to take me nearer to New Zealand; got one going to Tahiti. I arrived there in the middle of the night. Then we were told we would have to change planes again to take us on to New Zealand. It was amusing watching the cleaners coming in when it was still dark: we waited on the tarmac while little native girls with bare feet jumped vigorously all over the seats of the aeroplane dusting and cleaning. A most unusual sight. Not too many people were on the plane and we got to Auckland, New Zealand, round about midday. Everything was spotlessly clean in their airport. There were some nice little shops and I was able to buy a few knickknacks and phone Morag.

I told her I was taking yet another plane that would take me further up into North Island, nearer her home. She was astonished to hear my voice, as she had no idea I was coming. She got into her car and rapidly came to meet me as I alighted from my last aeroplane onto a country airstrip with the perfume of lupins coming into my nostrils. A lovely sensation, the air felt like champagne, maybe because I'd been drinking so much of it! I was impressed with the freshness, the sound of birds singing and the perfume of these flowers growing wild everywhere.

Morag's home was near a little country village called Opatama. A farm, one storey high but very elongated, it was in fact several houses put together and surrounded by tall poplar trees, a most romantic spot set in the middle of vast acres of fields. They were at the time breeding Black Angus cattle and sheep. The sheep looked more like teddy bears and I was astonished to see the hillsides yellow in colour, scorched with the sun. I'd left Britain in November and New Zealand was just beginning its summer, the earth was pretty scorched. I saw lots of goats and there was a river nearby Morag's home, with floating oil barrels and a rope going across for the milk to be brought from the neighbouring farm. All very primitive and strange. Trust me to arrive at a rather awkward time for Morag and Nigel; they were having that same evening a party and were busy hanging lanterns in the trees. There would be six barbecues going at the one time, all kinds of people coming, including the mayor, entertainment and dancing from the Maori girls, and a Maori piper. A great feast was to take place. I felt in the way.

So I asked them for a sandwich, I got into my bikini and decided I would go for a swim in the river. Off I went. I had my swim and, smelling the sea not too far away, decided to make my way there before going home. I had a fence to climb and thought, 'I'll just jump over it.' I was wearing the cross Kazik had given me, it was never off my neck, and I was soaking wet. I leapt over the fence and was electrocuted. Not too seriously, but it might have been fatal, so I lay on my back in the grass to recover, quite still, for some considerable time, forgetting that the sun was blazing down. Of course I got thoroughly sunburnt! My skin was beginning to blister and I was a hideous sight. I made my way back to the house, everyone was terribly kind, put all sorts of medicines and balms over my skin, and tried to make up my face to look like a human being before the guests arrived.

There were many social occasions during my stay in New Zealand. We took in Christmas and New Year with the Maoris: amusing to see the men dressed up in fur boots, in weather you could cook eggs on the sand and play tennis all through the night. Exciting to watch the lovely Maori girls dancing and singing their songs. This was the time, too, when the Olympics were going to be held in New Zealand and the Queen's yacht *Britannia* arrived for the occasion. It so happened that Morag's husband Nigel, being a seafaring man, was a great buddy of the Admiral of the Queen's yacht, so he came to stay with his wife and son, and then returned the compliment by asking us to dinner on board the *Britannia*.

This was the most thrilling event I'd ever known. Fortunately, before leaving Britain I'd bought myself a rather splendid evening gown in Inverness and it was going to come in very useful. Morag, Nigel and myself all went to dine on board the *Britannia*. We had cocktails up on deck at first and then went below for a most sumptuous evening meal. There were flunkies standing behind every chair and every morsel was put very carefully onto our plates. The wine was good and the conversation better; it was wonderful to be shown round the Queen's yacht, into all the places you don't hear much about, her private sitting room, the big banqueting hall, and having things explained to us. There were four big silver galleons on the table, and the Admiral explained that one of them would be put in front of the most important guest, to whom the Queen would be saying a few words.

Apart from these more dazzling occasions our days would be spent sunbathing and swimming down on the Mohangue Bay, on the Hawke's Bay, a superb stretch with huge breakers rolling in onto the beach and long grass to lie in, sand-hills that were warm and comforting. You could bask yourself from all angles, get a wonderful tan. On cooler days I would spend time painting on plates or making smoky plates, as I did at home at Lusa. I found a market for them; my niece Rona Òg, who is called after me, would take them to the villages and to the little towns and flog them, getting three times the price I ever got at home. I mostly painted Maori chiefs and scenes, little black pigs and beautiful blossoms that grow out there, some of the Maori children so beautiful and so exciting to paint – I did rather well. Indeed I did so well that Morag and I decided we would go for a trip to the South Island.

So we motored off to catch the ship that sails between North Island and South Island. The trip takes about as long as going from the Scottish mainland to the Outer Isles. We had a cabin on board the *Rangatira*, a very big elderly ship I will tell more about later. We sailed all night and arrived at the South Island in the early hours of the morning. I wanted to see Christchurch because Mr Rigby, a friend of my mother in the old days in Hoylake, had been commissioned to come to New Zealand and do carvings on the pews of the Christchurch Cathedral. Sightseeing right down to Queenstown and back was thrilling. We spent a night in the St Joseph Hotel away up on the slopes of Mount Cook, a luxury hotel that exceeded anything I'd ever known.

After basking in the best kind of luxury for the most part of a year, I felt it was time I was heading for home. I had arranged to go back by sea, so Morag and Nigel saw me off on the Greek ship *Australias*. We went aboard, examined my cabin and we agreed it was rather shabby, small; and two other ladies were going to occupy it with me. I was very, very sad leaving New Zealand and wondered if I'd ever see Morag and Nigel again. I decided I would phone them at the first stop.

The first stop we made was the Fiji Islands. We all went ashore and I made a call to Morag in driving rain. I never knew anything like it – I was soaked to the skin in a very thin silk dress, and straw hat, and of course I got ill. Indeed, I got very ill. I had a patch on my lung and eventually landed in the ship's hospital, situated far for'ard in the very peak of the ship. I lay in my bunk in a feverish state thinking about Fiji and how much I had enjoyed the glimpse of it – the band playing on the pier in the rain, all the men seemed to have bare feet and were wearing dark-coloured kilts. In my ignorance I hadn't thought this could be worn anywhere else than Scotland. There were enormous markets with open stalls and every conceivable object being sold, from food to ornaments and clothes. I just had enough time to buy an umbrella I needed badly and a mat made of leaves for hanging on a wall; I was told the designs were painted with blood.

As I lay there tossing and turning in my bed another patient was brought in. She was the most extraordinary-looking creature, a Fijian, dark in skin, and she looked like a monkey. She was very swollen, all her limbs out like balloons and as soon as the nurse had gone from our little ward she started talking to me, beseeching me to hold her hand, talk to her. I was very embarrassed because I was rather frightened and feeling very ill myself. She then stretched her arms towards me, grabbed the corners of the sheets of my bed and in my delirium I thought, 'Oh my God, she's going to eat me,' because I had read stories years ago about how there were cannibals in Fiji. I was convinced in my feverish state I would be gobbled up at any moment! This went on for days and nights and was very distressing.

Then one day the doctor came in and created an awful upheaval. He started to say to the nurse that this patient, not me but this other one, should not have been let on board. She had no right to be there and it was too late now, we were more than five miles out, to return her to Fiji – she would quite certainly die. And saying all this within the woman's hearing. I thought it very cruel, I couldn't understand it really. As they were leaving the ward and going into the corridor, the Greek doctor kept shouting at the nurse, 'She'll die, you know, she'll die! And what's more she'll burst and flood the place!' A couple of days later the only English-speaking nurse came to me, a very pretty girl, very nice, and she said, 'Come, dear, I've put a chair in the corridor for you. I want you to sit there because I think something awful is going to happen with this woman.' So I did as she said and went and sat in the corridor. Then I heard a bit later that the woman had quite literally burst open. It was horrific. She died of course and presumably was buried at sea. It was the worst nightmare I had ever known.

And now there were gales and stormy seas. Australia came and went, Mexico came and went, and eventually the *Australias* made her way to Southampton. The doctors were eager to get me ashore. I wondered why they were quite so eager but afterwards realised I was extremely ill. Loudspeakers were bleating out my name on the docks, asking if there was anyone

meeting me or related to me, and would they kindly come
forward? It was all very nerve-racking and then an ambulance
was summoned. I was shunted into that together with all my
luggage, not that I was trying to avoid going through customs
– oh no, but it is a jolly good way to avoid them! Everything
was piled in with me and stowed away in the Southampton
hospital when I got there.

I was put into intensive care and treated very well. Then I
was put into a smaller ward with just two other people for
about seven weeks and every kindness was shown to me. I
communicated with Catherine, Morag's second daughter. She
came and took me home to Kent, looked after me so well for
quite a long time, and then when I was stronger she took me
up to Euston Station in London, and put me on the sleeper. I
would make my way back to my beloved Isle of Skye, see again
the ancient Castle Moil. I would smell the imaginary peat
smoke coming out of the chimneys of all the small houses,
sadly no longer to be experienced. I would talk once again to
the mountains.

Instead of that I fell into the arms of my cousin Ena who
has the White Heather Hotel in Kyleakin, and she cared for
me so well. One thing about cousin Ena, she's always good
for a laugh. She had an amusing tale to tell; one day she'd
been in the kitchen scrubbing something or other when a
strange man came to the door wearing a turban and asking if
she could give tea to King Hussein and his wife and about
twenty of their retinue? Well, Ena was dumbfounded to say
the least of it.

Ena's Polish husband Vatzik had been up a ladder
mending part of the hotel roof, and Ena had dismissed
some of the staff (it being the end of the season) and was
sorting the linen herself, when in walked a tall man and

asked if it would be all right to bring in the king and queen?

'What king and queen?' says Ena.

'King Hussein of Jordan and his Queen, and their bodyguards, staff and attendants.'

'You're joking!' says Ena.

But no, he wasn't. He asked if he could look around and seemed well pleased with the dining room, even the bar, but asked if the ashtrays could be removed from the lounge before they came in. And she speedily did that and thought, 'Oh my God, I must get Vatzik!' Then they all came in, about four carloads, some in Arab costume – meanwhile, poor Ena in the middle of a hot flush tore outside to shout to Vatzik (see plate 25).

'Come off the roof! A king and queen are wanting tea and coffee so come down at once!'

'Don't be ridiculous,' replied Vatzik.

But he came all the same, and Ena told me that you could not have met nicer people: 'so natural', and they talked to all Ena's grandchildren, with little Laura getting special attention. 'No hal-de-dall about them,' says Ena.

King Hussein was charming to her and very interested in everything she was doing; the hotel, her children and grand-children.

That was only one of many exciting stories she had to tell, things that had been happening in my absence. But I only stayed with her a few days, I was longing to get back to Lusa. And when I did, it looked the same, completely unchanged, as it always had been. I was eager to settle down by the fire and chat once more to the phantom Katie, go to the whelks and once more follow the seagulls.

One fine day not long after returning to Lusa, having made myself a pot of my favourite onion soup, I decided to sit and enjoy it when there was a knock at the door.

'Come in!' I yelled.

In stepped a very tall, very handsome airman in uniform and he said, 'Terribly sorry to disturb you, but could I use your telephone? My plane is on the runway and there is nobody in the office. I can't get a key or anything to get access to the phone, and I am expecting to meet a lady from Barra, take her through to Edinburgh by plane.'

'Oh,' I said, 'go ahead.'

'Well,' he said, 'trouble is I haven't got any money.'

'Well,' I said, 'that's all right, I'll stand you the call, as it's an emergency.'

And so he made his call; I didn't listen. And then he said, 'My golly, that smells good.'

'Oh, my onion soup, I'm famous for it,' I said. 'Would you like to try it?'

And he said, 'Gosh, I'd love to, I'm absolutely starving.' So he sat and wolfed down the soup, obviously enjoying it. So we talked for a bit and he told me he was an independent person, running his own plane, could go anywhere he wanted. It was a wonderful life. He then said, 'Having enjoyed your company and soup, is there anywhere I can fly you? I can take you anywhere you like. Would you like me to fly you over to Edinburgh? We could drop down on Princes Street, it might be rather fun!'

So I thought, 'I wonder if I've got a nutcase here.' He didn't seem to be altogether barmy and so I said, 'Well, it so happens I've had a letter from my sister in New Zealand. She tells me that the ship which we sailed on together from North Island to South Island, the *Rangatira*, has sailed all the way, six thousand miles from New Zealand, and has made fast in, of all the places, in Kishorn! You can see Kishorn from here.' And I took him to the window and pointed out where the new rig opposite Skye was being made for the oil company. I said, 'That's where she lies, and is used as a sort of hotel, I believe. Now my sister says in her letter, "I want you to go, for old time's sake, and salute the *Ranagatira*!" 'And how can I do that?' I said, 'unless you would like to fly me over the area and I could salute her from the air!'

'Oh good idea,' he said. So we started to walk across the field, got over the river, and down to the airstrip which as I said before runs right up to the Pulpit Rock. So I got into this tiny little plane which just had two seats in it and he said, 'Now I'll take her up and then I'll give the controls over to you, you can steer any way you want.' So this we did. I was terrified really, but it seemed easy enough and I had my full sight then.

So we flew over Kishorn and I saw the *Rangatira* once again, was very thrilled indeed. When we got back this pilot offered to give me further lessons in flying, but I thought enough was enough and in any case when we were descending I had felt distinctly dizzy and sick. I didn't think it was a sport I would like to continue with so I said goodbye to him.

Then, later on, I was told that the *Rangatira* had been used in the Battle of the Falklands. She sure is a brave ship, and I'm proud to have sailed on her. So, I settled back in Lusa, and exchanged reminiscences with Katie once again.

Glossary of Gaelic and Scots

ag	– diminutive ending (G)
aran coirc	– oatcakes
bahookey	– arse
bairns	– children
beinn	– mountain top
big house	– main dwelling of an estate
blaggart	– blockhead cf bladair (G)
bodach	– old or churlish man
buidseach	– spell
C of Es	– Church of England members
cailleach	– old, single woman
carissamo	– my darling
céilidh	– visit to enjoy company
clootie	– dumpling wrapped in cloth and boiled
Eachan	– Hector
eightsome	– square set of four couples in Highland dancing
eilean	– island, isle
ENSA	– Entertainments National Service Association
fank	– sheepfold
gairm	– cockerel
horo-gheallaidh	– hullabaloo
hurling	– dashing in a speeding vehicle
jeelie-pan	– brass pot for making jam or jelly
Kuala Lumpur	– in Malaysia, in the Indian Ocean
long johns	– men's long-legged underwear
machair	– grasslands above shoreline
marag	– beef blood pudding
Maroons, The	– lifeboat crew at Mallaig
mór	– big; old
rudha	– promontory
Seumas	– James
sgian dubh	– black-hilted dagger
Sgitheana(i)ch	– Isle of Skye native

shevass	– seabhas (G) wandering
stirret	– wire mesh cage for roasting oatcakes
stravaig	– srabhaiche (G) like a straw, squandering (time)
Taillear, an	– the Tailor
tight	– tipsy, drunk
tishied	– walked affectedly cf titivate
Tormod	– Norman
torrnaig	– torran (G) little hill; bum (posterior)
trust	– trus-àite (G) wardrobe, settle
ultima Thule	– extreme limit of travel and discovery; the northern edge of the world (L)
VE Day	– World War II armistice, victory celebration
wee Free	– member of the Free Church of Scotland
winkle	– whelk (pejorative)